Raid on Port Royal

By

Perry Comer

Copyright (c) 2015 by Perry Comer

Warning: The unauthorized reproduction or distribution of this copyrighted work is illegal. Criminal copyright infringement, including infringement without monetary gain, is investigated by the FBI and is punishable by up to 5 (five) years in federal prison and a fine of $250,000.

Names, characters and incidents depicted in this book are products of the author's imagination or are used fictitiously. Any resemblance to actual events, locales, organizations, or persons, living or dead, is entirely coincidental and beyond the intent of the author or the publisher.

No part of this book may be reproduced or transmitted in any form or by any means, electronic or mechanical, including photocopying, recording, or by any information storage and retrieval system, without permission in writing from the publisher.

DEDICATION

Jerry Jones

More than a brother-in-law

BOOKS BY PERRY COMER (Allan Brooks)

The Prize
(Donland)

The Messenger
Donland and the Hornet

Donland's Ransom
Donland and the Hornet

Raid on Port Royal
Donland and the Hornet

The Bond of Duty
Donland and the Hornet

Seige
Donland and The Hornet

The Rescue
Donland and the Hornet

The Snake Killer
(Juvenile Action/adventure)

God's Broken Man
(Allan Brooks) (Christian Fiction)

Myrtle Beach Murder
(Allan Brooks)(Christian Fiction)

Fall of Fort Fisher
(Juvenile action/adventure)
(Civil War)

Andrew's War
(Juvenile action/adventure)
(Civil War)

Fighting Marines: Hardy's Commission

Fighting Marines: Hardy's Challenge

BACKGROUND

THE PRIZE (first book in the series)

Isaac Donland was born to Presbyterian missionary parents in Pennsylvania. He became an orphan when Indians attacked and killed his parents. Rescued by a trapper, he was placed first with a millwright and then a ship's chandler. A lieutenant, son of an admiral, befriended him and brought him aboard his ship as a cabin boy. Seeing courage and willingness in young Donland, the admiral sponsored him as a midshipman.

Serving an as second lieutenant aboard the frigate *Medusa* Donland is given charge of a captured French Frigate to be delivered to Antigua. The ship is badly holed and has temporary repairs. Master's Mate Jackson is assigned as first lieutenant and Donland is ordered to deliver a badly wounded boy named David along with his man-servant, Samson.

Donland is forced to beach *Morgador* after an encounter with a French frigate. With a crew of thirty they set about the task of making repairs and refloating the ship. An American privateer attempts to enter the small cove where *Morgador* is beached and Donland captures her. Aboard is a captive, by the name of Betty Sumerford.

Donland and his party survive a mutiny, hurricane and another attack by the French. Sailing from the island to Antigua, he falls in love with Betty. For his bravery and dedication he is advanced to commander and given the sloop *Hornet.*

THE MESSENGER (second book in the series)

Hornet was a cursed ship. Distrust of the fever-laden *Hornet* and the young American born Captain are an ill fit to the fleet of Admiral Hyde-Parker and Admiral Rowley. Yet, a small squadron of Spanish ships hampers their communications and *Hornet* is given the task of running the gauntlet. Trapped and outgunned, he must use his wits to escape and keep the dispatches he is carrying from falling into the hands of the Spanish. From Charles Town to Martinique, Donland faces storms, treachery and envy. In time he accepts his role. Jackson put it into perspective, "Would you rather be fourth on that hulk yonder or be the messenger boy for the fleet."

DONLAND'S RANSOM (Third Book)

Goya looked to the right and then to the left." Do you surrender or no?"

Sumerford surprised Donland by saying, "We have information concerning the kidnapped Prince. Once we see the Counsel, we will depart."

Goya was a calculating man. It showed in his bearing and in his eyes." You are in no position to ask anything or bargain. You are now my prisoners and this vessel is property of Spain. You will disarm your men or be fired upon."

Pirates capture the crown prince of Portugal. Donland is to deliver five hundred pounds, a king's ransom, to an unnamed man in Grenada. The man has requested Donland and the *Hornet* to deliver the money and to provide assistance to freeing the prince. Admiral Rowley tells him that the French and the Spanish will seek to gain the prince so that Portugal will be sympathetic to their cause of defeating England. Should Donland fail to gain the prince's release it will go hard on him and not the man whose plan it is to rescue the prince.

Historical Information

The Battle of Port Royal Island, Feb. 3, 1779

The Colonials won by default. Interesting was the fact that the battle was fought with the British forces hiding and firing from behind trees while the Colonials marched across a grassy meadow. The British, for some reason, withdrew, leaving the field of battle to the Colonials. There were few deaths and few wounded, but it was hailed as a victory for the Colonial militia.

The Battle of Grenada took place on 6 July 1779

Admiral Byron and his fleet chased and fought the French fleet of Comte D'Estaing. Before this battle there was a great deal of speculation about the Spanish and the Portuguese augmenting the French fleet. The battle ended in a defeat for the British, even without the assistance of other forces.

James Boyd - Kettle Creek

James Boyd was an Irish immigrant to South Carolina prior to the revolution. He rose to Colonel and often functioned in the role of spy for the British Loyalists. Sir Henry Clinton of New York devised a plan to raise up forces in the Carolinas and Georgia to retake territory lost to the Colonials. Boyd was assigned the task of raising those forces. Boyd's forces fought the Colonials at Kettle Creek, Georgia and were routed. Boyd died.

Chapter One

Donland was summoned to the flagship to meet with Flag Captain Calder at four in the afternoon. The midshipman sent to fetch him was a freckled-face thin boy of perhaps twelve. He was a fair-haired little waif, smaller than David. Donland was surprised the youngest was allowed out on his own. But as he reflected, he was not more than this boy when he was serving as cabin boy and often sent alone on errands.

Captain Calder was waiting. "Time is short commander," he said and rose from his desk with a packet in his hand. "You are to proceed to Antigua. We have urgent dispatches and you will have three passengers; Captain Milton Lyons, a clergyman name of Dundas and Mister Sumerford. Pay no heed to Captain Lyons as he is not well. He was wounded and his wound causes him great distress. The fleet surgeon has ordered him back to England to regain his health."

Donland said nothing, but knew that having a post captain even as a passenger might prove difficult and hinder his command.

"Here are the dispatches," Calder said, handing over the packet. As to Captain Lyons, he is under the care of Dundas so he should cause you no difficulties. They will have your cabin and Sumerford can manage as you direct. Are you ready to sail?"

"Aye Sir," Donland answered.

"One other thing, your reports," Calder said as he returned to his chair and sat. He picked up a sheaf of papers. "These are reports I have received today from other captains. Most are laborious, wordy and of little substance. I go through a stack of these each day and my eyes grow weary and my brain is numbed from the receptiveness of the same tired phrases and flowery prose." He dropped the sheaf of papers and extracted a single sheet. "You, of course, recognize this?"

"Aye Sir, it is one of my reports."

Donland felt very uneasy about the report. He could recall nearly every word of it. The blasted thing had taken the better part of a day to write and re-write until he was satisfied with the contents.

Calder gave a tight smile. "Most captains on this station would have written ten or more pages to convey what you have written on less than a full page. Your brevity and your clarity are commendable. I would that all captains would be so direct with their reports. Unfortunately for me, they will not. I must wade through the muck of many details that have nothing at all to do with actions and reactions. It is as if these captains have nothing better to do than fill paper with their triviality. I confess to being harsh to a few of your rank and scold them." He smiled broadly and continued, "And here I am wasting breath to thank you for being concise and to the point. The fewer the words the better, eh?"

Again Donland was not sure how to reply.

Calder must have seen the wheels turning and the confusion in Donland's eyes. "Commander Donland just say thank you sir and return to your ship."

Sheepishly Donland managed, "Thank you Sir."

Donland mulled over the meeting with Calder as he was rowed back to *Hornet.* Jackson was waiting on deck. Donland saluted the flag and said to him, "We sail on the morning tide, Mister Jackson. We are to make a quick passage to English Harbor with three passengers who will be coming out to us before nightfall. Let us shift our dunnage to accommodate them."

"One is aboard already Sir; Mister Sumerford is in your cabin."

"Aye, he would be," Donland mused. "There will be a bumboat with provisions within the hour. Since my cabin will be occupied, have the boxes stored in the bread locker if you please."

"Aye Captain," Jackson replied.

"I'm going below, I do not want to be disturbed," Donland stated as he put a foot on the hatch ladder.

Sumerford stood with his hands clasped behind his back staring out the stern windows.

"Matthias I must say I'm not surprised that you are sailing with us," Donland stated as he crossed to shake Sumerford's hand.

"No one I would rather entrust my life to," Sumerford said as he turned.

"And I would take it that your sailing is not by chance?"

"Indeed it is not by chance. My presence is required or it would be my head."

He took Sumerford's bait. "I doubt your head is in danger, it would seem that mine is of less value than yours and sooner parted than yours."

"About that," Sumerford began. "Trust is a commodity

that is expensive to buy. As I explained, I had need of a man I could trust and one with a cool head and sharp wits. The sum of money entrusted to you and the task of retrieving Prince Dom Joao required such a man, and you proved yourself not only to me but to Captain Calder and Admiral Hyde-Parker. It is unfortunate that it was deemed necessary for you to be the scapegoat if things went awry. But, such was for naught for you, dear boy, preformed brilliantly and pleased not just admirals but I'm sure even the Nabobs. Now let's have a drink!"

Sumerford lifted a bottle of port from the table.

"No!" Donland said firmly. "Your smooth tongue dances well around what is unsaid because it suits your purposes. Even if it causes harm to those who needed to know. Captain Calder only this day heaped praise on my report writing for being direct and concise. So I shall be such with you, why are you aboard *Hornet*?"

Sumerford continued pouring wine into two glasses. "That is direct, but I'll not share that information at this time." He handed Donland a glass." I can tell you that we shall be spending considerable time together and that you will need your mittens."

Donland was about to ask if they were going to Boston from Antigua, but refrained as Sumerford pointed toward the skylight.

"To your good health, Isaac," Sumerford toasted.

Captain Lyons, a tall man over six feet thin in waist and shoulders, came aboard *Hornet* before sunset. His dunnage was astonishingly meager for a post captain.

He was piped aboard with all the ceremony befitting his rank and standing. However, Lyons neither doffed his hat nor returned Donland's salute. Donland saw only a portion of the man's face wrapped as he was in a heavy coat with the collar turned up to his ears. Dundas, with the aid of a younger man not in uniform, guided Lyons below.

"Ah there you are Captain Donland. I was just on my way to see you with a small request for Captain Lyons," Dundas said as he returned to the deck.

Upon first meeting, Donland did not care for Dundas. Self-important men riding the coattails of greater men were always an irritation to him. Dundas was one of the worst he had encountered. The man, short in stature, was puffed up, not only in his self-estimate but in his belly as well.

"Good morning, Reverend Dundas. What is your small request?" Donland managed as pleasantly as he could.

"It's the matter of the ship's biscuits, sir. Might it be possible to have someone inspect them for weevils before being served to Captain Lyons? He does so detest them. I myself find them to be of no bother but the poor Captain, the sight of them repels him."

Donland smiled, knowing Captain Lyons had not the wit about him to make such a request. Even so, being a man given to the sea, he would have not considered a weevil a problem were he in his right mind.

"Aye, they will be checked. Now sir if you will please see to Captain Lyons," Donland said dismissing the man.

Dundas did not reply, instead curtly spinning on his heel and disappeared down the hatch.

"One day of sailing and double the irritation I take it," Sumerford said.

"Aye," Donland answered. "Another day and we shall be in English Harbor and done with this lot."

"Done with this lot and to take on another, perhaps even more difficult to pacify," Sumerford said.

Donland did not miss the hint. "It would be my misfortune to have a bevy of skirted females to ferry to Charles Town or onward to Boston."

"Misfortune Captain, I'd not call it a misfortune; more of a reward for dependable faithful service," Sumerford suggested and smiled a cat-like smile. "But Boston, no, you'd not be that fortunate."

Donland considered Sumerford's statement along with the smile. He concluded from Sumerford's statement that their destination was not to be Boston but Charles Town.

"Whither thou goest," he mocked Sumerford by citing the Book of Ruth.

"Aye, thy people shall be my people," Sumerford replied finishing the verse.

Donland grinned but did not reply.

"What is that island off the bow to starboard?" Sumerford asked.

"Montserrat," Donland answered, fully aware that Sumerford was deliberately changing tack. The man did not want to answer as to their destination or to his affairs. Secrets and lies seemed to be the stock in trade of Sumerford as it was with those who served the crown in less than honorable ways. He wondered if it troubled his friend. *Friend!* He had surprised himself thinking of Sumerford as such.

In the forenoon watch the hail came.

"Deck there! Sail to starboard three points!"

Donland heard the hail. He glanced up from the purser's log resting on his knees. In his mind's eye he pictured the requisite chart. *Hornet* was well west of Guadeloupe and just south of Montserrat. It was likely that the sail was from Antigua and likely an English frigate on patrol. He continued with Jones' log.

"Frigate!" The lookout shouted down.

A breath later the man called, "Another frigate trailing!"

The captain of the first frigate would no doubt draw near for a closer inspection and might order *Hornet* to heave-to. There was nothing for it but to don coat and hat and await signals.

As his head emerged from the hatchway, he noted that *Hornet*'s number was already flying overhead, as was the ensign.

"No recognition signal, Captain!" Jackson reported as Donland approached.

Donland took the glass Jackson offered and found the frigate charging ahead of *Hornet* on a western tack. She was hull down, less than four miles out. She had an ensign flying but no other flags.

"Thirty-two guns!" He said aloud.

The second frigate also had her ensign aloft and flags were run up as Donland studied her. *Hornet's* number! *Give chase*!

He studied the first frigate again for several seconds. There was no indication that she desired to communicate or acknowledge *Hornet.* He did not hesitate." Sound the bell if you please, Mister Jackson! Beat to quarters!"

The clanging of the bell calling the watches to their stations set off an orderly chaos. Men threw themselves into preparing *Hornet* to engage the enemy. Petty officers urged the men to their stations with starters, oaths and a few kicks to slow moving backsides. The decks were sanded, fire parties took their stations at the pumps and gunners unleashed their weapons in preparation of priming.

He estimated the speed of the frigate racing ahead. She was close-hauled but would no doubt tack northward once clearing Montserrat. By so doing she would attempt to gain more distance from her pursuer. *Hornet*, however, was running with the wind and could trail in the frigate's wake when she tacked. But prior to that tack, *Hornet* would be in the range of her guns.

"The Frog is running for his life," Jackson mused.

"Aye," Donland said and added," The captain of that frigate pursuing would have us shorten his life. But in so doing we might end ours."

Jackson observed, "He's close-hauled and can tack and then have the wind up his arse."

"Aye," Donland agreed and added while nodding toward the English frigate, "The hound must contend with the island before tacking. By the time he does we shall either be taking the tiger by the tail or swimming."

The gamble was great, but the reward could be greater. If *Hornet* could damage the fleeing frigate, then the English frigate could catch her and take her. It was a gamble, and it was time to decide. "Helm two points starboard!" Donland ordered.

"Belay that order!" Captain Lyons shouted as he struggled against Dundas who was holding to his arm.

"Sir! Sir! We must go below," Dundas was shouting as he tugged at the much larger Captain Lyons.

"Blast your eyes! I'll have you flogged around the fleet!" Lyons shouted at Dundas. Spittle and foam came from his mouth.

Samson appeared as if by magic behind Lyons and Dundas. Scooping Lyons up in his giant arms, Samson flung the man over his shoulder. Taking giant strides, Samson made for the hatchway.

Lyons could be heard shouting obscenities as Samson carried him down the steps. Dundas followed.

Donland watched them go, blew a breath and faced toward the fleeing frigate.

"Mister Jackson, we will close the gap a bit more. When the Frenchman begins his tack, we shall follow."

"Mister Aldridge, take a glass and watch for the slightest change on the deck of that frigate. Call out when you see men muster."

"Aye Captain!" Aldridge replied.

Donland shouted, "Mister Andrews lay aft if you please!"

Andrews obeyed and hurried aft.

"Mister Andrews load the larboard guns with chain-shot.

Maximum elevation! We shall lay onto the Frenchman's wake when he tacks and stay on his starboard quarter. As those guns bear fire and load, don't wait for orders. I want you to disable as much of his rigging as you can."

"Aye Sir!" Andrews replied.

"Set the royals, Mister Jackson if you please, a knot or more will not come amiss," Donland ordered.

"Stuns'l booms rigged out, sir?" Jackson asked.

"Aye Mister Jackson."

Hornet surged forward, aided by the press of sail and a slight strengthening of wind. There was no doubt that they were coming up quickly on the frigate.

"Ports opening, Sir!" Aldridge shouted.

Donland was not surprised. He would have done the same if he were being chased. A chance hit on a sloop pursuing would slow and perhaps deter the smaller vessel.

The Frenchman yawed and fired two of his guns, probably eight-pounders. Both balls were wide of *Hornet* and short.

"Captain!" Aldridge shouted.

"Mister Dewitt starboard three points!" Donland called. "Put us on her stern and follow!"

"Aye Captain!" Dewitt called.

"Mister Jackson we shall outpace her!"

Jackson began ordering changes to sail to maximize the use of wind.

Donland put the glass he was holding to his eye to check on the progress of the English frigate. Her sails bellowed and the curtain of her bow wave suggested that her captain was intent upon catching his quarry. He studied her several seconds longer and counted twenty guns. The Frenchman was the *Concorde* armed with thirty-two guns.

"The *Ariadne*, Captain Thomas Pringle," Dewitt said from behind.

"Aye," Donland replied. In his mind it would be an even fight by British standards.

Concorde's tack brought her onto the wind. Donland could visibly see that they were closing the distance at an alarming rate. By the time *Concorde* finished her tack, *Hornet* would be in her range.

The *Ariadne* was several minutes from being clear of the island and able to tack. *Hornet* had to buy her that time.

"Two points more to starboard Mister Dewitt if you please!"

"Mister Andrews as you bear!" Donland shouted.

Hornet seemed to be flying; overhead the rigging was singing. Dewitt held course and *Hornet* was running in the frigate's wake. Everything seemed to be taking a great deal of time. Donland's attention was drawn alternately to the bowsprit and to the sails and then back again.

Boom! Boom!

Andrews had fired and Donland gave his full attention to the frigate's sails for any result.

Both shots fell short.

Hornet was still closing the distance.

"Prepare to reduce sail Mister Jackson when we've got the range!" Donland shouted.

Ariadne had yet to begin her tack.

"Signal Captain!" Aldridge shouted." Engage more closely!"

Donland smiled to himself. He was pressing the attack but he'd not get so close or be so cocky as to put *Hornet* in greater danger.

Boom!

Andrews' next shot tore into the *Concorde's* transom.

Boom!

The second shot ripped through her rigging and punctured a sail.

A shout went up from the crew. "Huzza Huzza!"

"Quiet there!" Donland yelled.

He studied the frigate to anticipate her next move. It came as no surprise. She yawed to starboard.

Three guns belched fire from forward on her gun deck. They were poorly and hastily laid, for all three shots went high and fell harmless to larboard.

Hornet's deck shook as her two guns fired again.

Donland smiled, Andrews had taken advantage of the larger target when *Concorde* yawed and fired the two guns. Both chained shots found their mark and the main t'gallant and tops'l of the Frenchman were shredded.

Again the cheers went up. Donland allowed them to cheer for they had achieved their task.

Jackson shouted, "Quiet there! Our work is just begun!"

Ariadne had made her tack, and she had every stitch of canvas drawing. The *Concorde* was wounded but not mortally. She still had the firepower to destroy *Hornet* and perhaps dispatch *Ariadne* as well.

"Mister Dewitt hold this course. Stay starboard of her quarter," Donland ordered.

"Mister Jackson reduce sail, pace her if you please!"

"Aye Captain aye!" Jackson answered and there was no mistake in his joy of the moment.

Donland knew now was the time to inflict the fatal blow that would allow *Ariadne* the opportunity to come alongside the *Concorde*. "Mister Andrews load with shot if you please. Fire into the transom, take out her rudder!"

Ariadne was gaining as the *Concorde* slowed. The hounds had the fox and to Donland's mind it was to be a bloody fight.

Boom!

He saw the flash and the smoke seconds before he heard the crash of the ball slam into the foremast. Instantly there was a shower of blocks, tackle and the twang of lines snapping. The *Concorde* had done the unexpected by shifting a heavy cannon round to the transom and fired. The shot was either well aimed or the French gunner had the greatest of luck.

Men screamed as they fell and as the top half of the

foremast came crashing down. Men stood stunned, others hurried to their injured messmates. Jackson rushed from the quarterdeck. "Clear that away!" He shouted to a gun crew.

"You men hack those lines! Get this rabble over the side." Jackson shouted to another gun crew.

The fallen sail instantly reduced *Hornet*'s speed and caused her to slew to larboard.

"Mister Dewitt bring her back on course!" Donland shouted.

Seeing Dawkins he ordered, "Take ten men forward and set them mending that rigging!"

Boom!

A second shot from the Concorde's transom blasted apart the *Hornet's* launch, sending splinters flying toward the helm. In an instant, Donland was down. He was unaware that Samson and Dewitt were also down.

The world went black for several long seconds before his vision returned. It was as if he was in a deep well and fought to see the light at the top. He saw only blue tinged with black at first and slowly he focused to see white sails overhead.

Jackson seeing the destruction raced along the deck leaping over fallen men, pieces of the launch and fallen blocks to get to the helm.

Donland was sitting up and was attempting to stand as Jackson reached him.

"*Hornet*, Mister Jackson, she comes first," Donland mumbled.

Jackson stood perplexed, torn between helping his captain and seeing to *Hornet's* needs.

His head began to clear. "That's an order, Mister Jackson!"

"Aye Captain!" Jackson replied and surveyed the deck.

"You there! See to the captain!" He shouted to a seaman intent on assisting a dead mate.

Donland attempted to stand, wobbled but stood. He put his hand into his coat and drew it away. There was no blood.

Something had struck him hard enough to knock him down and rob him of breath. *Probably broke a rib or two*, he thought. The pain was intense, but he would not give in to it. He turned his attention to *Concorde*; she was yawing again." Oh God!" He said in anticipation of a broadside.

Concorde fired a slow rolling broadside. He saw the flash and belch of the guns, but no ball crashed into *Hornet*. *Ariadne*, no doubt, was the intended target. Even as he struggled to twist about to see the fall of shot he heard the balls striking home. The screams of wounded men carried across the water. *Ariadne's* mizzen came down in a small cascade of canvas and rigging. It slid off the starboard side and began to drag the ship around. It was the way of the French, cripple the enemy first and deal with any survivors second.

"Luck!" Dewitt said as he took Donland's arm. "Bloody frogs can't shoot worth a damn and every jack knows it. Bloody luck!"

The sound of a boy crying caught Donland's attention. To his left he saw Samson, blood pooled around the big man's head. A large splinter was imbedded near his ear. David was on his knees holding Samson's dead lifeless hand. The boy sobbed with great anguish.

The roar of guns called Donland back to his duty. *Concorde* loosed another broadside in the direction of *Ariadne*. The smash and crash of the balls was lost in the ragged salvo unleashed by *Ariadne's* guns. All of her shots fell harmless in the sea, *Concorde* was untouched.

Captain Pringle had tried to wound the larger ship, but to no avail. *Ariadne's* sail and standing rigging were in shreds; there could be no pursuit, only the burials of her dead. Luck had not been on their side this day.

Donland put a hand on David's shoulder. "Mister Welles, there's naught you can do for him. We shall mourn later. Remember I told you, not this day, not this hour, for others depend on me!"

David looked up at him; his face was wet with tears. "Aye Sir, I remember."

"Others are depending on you, Mister Welles," Donland said gently.

"Aye Sir," David answered, stood and began wiping his tears with the sleeve of his coat.

Donland half-smiled. "Assist Mister Andrews if you please."

David stepped around Samson's body, glanced down, and then took a step. He turned, took one last look at his friend, then hurried away.

The pain caused Donland to wince. "Have we steerage Mister Dewitt?"

"Aye Sir," Dewitt answered.

"Very well, stay on her stern. We shall hit her again!"

"Aye Captain!" Dewitt replied with apprehension.

"Boom!" The gun in *Concorde's* transom fired again.

Hornet shuddered as the ball tore into the light timbers and through planking at the waterline near the starboard bow. The heavy ball crashed through a bulkhead, showering those below with more splinters.

"Mister Aldridge please go below and see to the damage!" Donland ordered the midshipman.

"Aye Captain!" Aldridge replied as if he wanted to be away from the death on deck.

"Helm's sluggish Captain!" Dewitt called.

Concorde was out distancing *Hornet*. Donland watched her. Her rigging was alive with men as they set the damaged rigging to rights. *Hornet* would not catch her and even if she did, it would be a fight they would lose. He watched her then turned aside; his ship needed him.

Donland called out loudly. "Mister Jackson top'sl's only! Keep steerage, but no more! I'll have a look below!"

Aldridge was coming up the hatchway as Donland descended. "Water is pouring in Sir!" Aldridge stated and there was no mistaking the fear in his voice.

"Fetch the bosom and his mates. Have the pumps manned!" Donland ordered as he hurried on to view the damage.

The hole was a gaping hole, but it was not the immediate threat. Below the hole the seams had given way and water was pouring in. The bilge and the holds were filling quickly. The pumps would not be able to keep up. He raced up the hatchway.

"Mister Dewitt hard over to larboard!"

"Mister Jackson take in all sail, we will lay to!"

"Mister Andrews detail a party and fodder a sail over the starboard bow! Draw it tight across the bottom!"

Chapter Two

A squall washed over *Hornet,* rinsing away the blood but not the cries of the wounded. Men worked aloft, the foremast was being fished. There was no joviality; the men went about their work with dogged determination. They had barely begun to fight when the fight was over. Mates lay dead, others maimed for life. The pumps were manned and keeping pace with the many leaks. *Hornet* would survive.

Ariadne's surgeon, a tall gaunt man named Morris, came aboard *Hornet* an hour before sunset. He went first to the seriously wounded on the orlop. Two limbs required removal; several of the men required splinters to be plucked from torsos and a few other men required bandaging. He then went up to Donland.

"Captain I find no breaks but that is not to say there are none as I'm very poor at seeing through uncut flesh. I shall bind your ribs and they should mend in a few weeks. You'll not be dashing up the rigging, I dare say."

It was good news and such was in short supply. *Hornet* had lost four men and eleven were wounded. *Ariadne* had lost sixteen killed and twenty-eight wounded. All in all they counted themselves lucky to be alive. *Concorde* chose to continue north rather than stay and finish the two smaller ships. It would have been a bloody fight and the *Concorde* would no doubt have suffered more damage. Whatever the Frenchman's reasoning, he chose to haul his wind.

"Mister Andrews I will make a favorable note in my log of your gunnery," Donland said as he inspected the gun lashings.

Andrews face shown with pleasure. "Thank you kindly Captain. We would have had her Sir were it not for that gun in her transom. My lads would have put a few more right into her and that's no err. Pity we've not done so sooner and took out that gun."

Donland nodded. "Almost but not quite Mister Andrews. I would hazard to guess that the moment we came onto his wake that French captain ordered the gun moved and they set about rigging the tackles. Your first shot probably killed a few of the gun crew otherwise he would have had us dead to rights earlier."

Andrews seemed to consider what Donland had said, then answered, "Aye."

"The French captain is a cunning man. We'll do well to remember that the next time we engage him," Donland said and continued to inspect *Hornet*'s damage.

Sumerford stood amidships looking out at the empty sea. He seemed oblivious to the work going on around him as men scurried to make and mend.

"Something troubling you Mathias?" Donland asked.

"Time troubles me Captain. Seems there is either not enough or too much."

"You are in a hurry to reach Boston?"

"That would be your assumption," Sumerford replied.

"Ever fishing for what is in my mind aren't you?"

"Only as far as it concerns *Hornet.* And, I've no doubt that your plans involve her."

Sumerford changed tack. "Sorry about your man Samson."

"Aye. Thank you for that," Donland answered then added. "I shall not see his like again."

Donland assembled the ship's company. There were four bodies on the gratings shrouded in their hammocks. A round shot had been sewn into each of the hammocks. It was a sad affair and a first for several members of the company. They would not soon forget.

He removed the whistle from his pocket and blew a blast. All became still and silent. He opened his Bible and began to read from the eleventh chapter of John. Then he read the first three verses of the fourteenth chapter of John. He concluded by saying, "It is our sad duty to now commit the bodies of our mates to the deep."

As he called each name, Samson Freeman, Jonas McBee, Natawasi and Ezra Smith, the grating was lifted and the body slid into the sea with a splash. Donland again blew the whistle signaling the end of the burial service.

The men drifted away to their stations and duties. As they went, Donland put an arm around David's shoulder and pulled him close. It was a small show of affection and one he would not have given any other. Samson had been like the boy's uncle and sometimes like his father. The two had endured much and there was never any doubt of the bond of love between them. The boy was alone in the world now save for Donland.

David had managed to stand without shaking or trembling as Samson's body went over. His face was still wet with tears but he had not sobbed.

He released the boy's shoulder. "Mister Welles, if you please, my cabin is in disarray. Take Simon below and supervise. Set things to rights if you please."

It was still light as Thomas Pringle was rowed across to *Hornet*. Pringle was a powerfully built man in his late forties. He was as tall as Donland but seemed much larger.

He came aboard to the twitter of the whistle and the stamp of the marines. "I'll not be long Captain Donland as I've much to attend to. My surgeon told me of your wounds and that it was best that you not make the crossing to *Ariadne*. We're knocked about a bit by that Frenchie. By God, he was lucky. Five more minutes and I'd had him in the bag."

"Aye Sir," Donland agreed.

"That devil has been playing havoc with our supplies and communications. We've not seen the last of him, of that I'm certain. I shall set off after him at first light and he'll not escape a good thrashing." He paused then asked, "You have orders for English harbor? Dispatches?"

"Aye Sir." Donland answered.

"More's the pity. I could use more eyes and more guns. I must get back across. I shall send my reports for the admiral and some personal letters in an hour or so. Be so kind as to show a light that my midshipman might find you without getting lost. His father would not forgive me if I could not give and accounting."

"Aye Sir," Donland replied.

As darkness overtook *Hornet* and *Ariadne* lanterns were hung in the rigging. The sound of hammers and saws continued well into the night before ceasing near midnight. Pringle's midshipman came and went without being lost. Aboard both vessels some men took occasion to get drunk from the stores of fermented spirits they had hidden. More than one toast was offered to dead shipmates so recently confined to the deep. Sad music played on mouth harps and fiddles.

Donland heard the tunes, his soul was melancholy.

Memories of Samson entered his consciousness on more than one occasion. Twice he had called for him only to be reminded that Samson lay beneath the waves.

Sometime in the night the lanterns aboard *Ariadne* were extinguished. She slipped away either by tide or sail to resume her chase of *Concorde.*

Donland was finishing his breakfast of biscuit, salt pork and water when Dundas appeared wringing his hands.

"He would like to speak with you Captain," Dundas said.

"In a while Reverend Dundas," Donland replied as he rose from the table and wiped his mouth.

"Sir, later may not be a good time," Dundas implored. "For the moment he is in a decent frame of mind. I fear it'll not last."

Donland considered the request. "Aye, I'll come."

Captain Lyons was sitting with his back to the cabin staring out the transom at *Hornet's* wake.

"You wanted to see me Captain Lyons?" Donland asked.

Lyons stood and faced Donland. He was smiling and said, "I do indeed. We've not had the occasion, because of my sickness, to converse. I've only just come to know that I'm aboard your ship and have been for several days. Reverend Dundas, my jailer whom I detest, informed me that I caused you more than a little trouble. I do apologize for my outburst and for difficulties I have caused you."

"You've caused no great trouble Captain Lyons," Donland assured him.

"Ah, but I have and I've a memory of being on your deck in the midst of a fight. It was not right, sick or no, it was not right. A captain is master of every plank and peg, man and boy. There's no room for another. Don't you agree?"

"Aye Sir."

"Therefore I owe you my apology. It will not happen again."

"Accepted Sir and thank you Sir," Donland managed

wanting to be away and to his duties.

Lyons must have sensed Donland's unease and said, "Youth is wasted on the young. They've not time for apologies nor for old men. I know for I well remember my own youth, I've not much else left to me but fleeting memories." He paused and turned to stare out at the sea for a moment then turned again to Donland. "The haze that clouds my mind comes and goes, it will return at any moment so hear me out. I do apologize with all my heart for causing you troubles. Your tolerance has been a virtue and a kindness I'll cling to, as I'm able. Accept what I say to you as a kindness and not as meddlesome. In his majesty's service there are those who care not what you suffer and they will abuse you. Their orders may be lawful but those orders may be for their purposes only and not for the good of you, your ship or for the king. Do not go blindly nor trusting in all you are commanded. Old men only get to be old because they learn to step lightly, speak only as they hear and see beyond what is on the horizon."

Lyons was about to say more but his face contoured in a spasm of pain. When it passed, Lyons eyes were glassy, questioning.

Donland turned and opened the door to leave.

"I did not give you permission to leave! Blast your eyes! Marines arrest that man!" Lyons shouted.

Dundas pushed past Donland.

Hornet seemed to be racing on the wind. She was slightly heeled to starboard. Her bowsprit jutting forward raising and falling, pointing toward English Harbor. Donland wondered what fate Lyons would have once reaching there and what awaited him in England should he reach there. It was true; there were worse fates than death.

Chapter Three

Lieutenant Barnes, flag lieutenant for Admiral Rowley came aboard *Hornet* just after dawn to escort Captain Lyons ashore. The man was curt and not at all sympathetic towards Captain Lyons. He afforded Dundas more attention than the man deserved which annoyed Donland more than a little.

Donland mustered the side party for the captain's departure. He felt Lyons was due the honor. Many may forget the man's achievements and his service but he would not.

Barnes other purpose for coming to *Hornet* was to inform Donland that Admiral Rowley would see him at nine at his residence.

"You will know it at once because it is the two-story house with blue shutters," Barnes stated.

Donland had seen the house and knew that on the bottom floor there was a drinking room where young officers drank and gambled. The upper level was until recently a brothel. It was the same house he had once found Andrews.

He was not surprised to find that the house with the blue shutters was no longer a brothel and there were no young lieutenants in the drinking room. Admiral Rowley had taken over the house and re-furnished the downstairs. The hallway contained two long wooden benches without upholstery. A young clerk with bushy sideburns and long stringy black hair sat at a small desk.

"Commander Donland," He announced himself.

"Through there," the clerk pointed with a bony finger to a doorway covered with a drapery.

Admiral Rowley sat behind a very plain desk much unlike the one aboard the flagship. He was blunt, "I have orders for *Hornet*, they will be brought to you day after tomorrow as I have to complete some details. I can tell you that you will act as transport for the army. I am giving you command over two other vessels that will be laden with powder, shot, arms and stores. These are to be landed near Port Royal in Carolina. You will need to provision your ships for the cruise and possibly for a week or more lying-to."

Pausing, the Admiral studied Donland quietly for a second before continuing.

"There has been some discussion as to whether or not you are the right man to undertake this cruise," he said then paused studying Donland.

"I believe," he continued, "your first lieutenant is a colonist as is the master?"

"Aye Sir," Donland answered and felt ill at ease because of the question.

"And, you yourself are also one?"

"Aye Sir, I was born a New Englander."

Admiral Rowley adjusted himself in his chair, crossing his legs. "The cruise you are to undertake, against the concerns of some, is to deliver the troops and materials as I said, to colonists loyal to the crown. The concern is, can you be trusted to do so?" He held up a hand to stop Donland from answering. "I believe you will and do so with a clear conscience. Your actions of late speak to that belief. Have I mis-stated?"

"No Sir, I wear the King's coat and do so willingly."

"Very good?" Admiral Rowley said as he uncrossed his legs. He picked up a page from his desk. "Lieutenant Powell commands *Stinger* and Lieutenant Newland commands Jacket. Are you acquainted with these men?"

"Powell yes, Newland only just."

Admiral Rowley nodded and explained, "Both were only recently promoted to commander and that makes you senior. I'm told the sloops are seaworthy and their companies are untried as well as under-manned. It will fall to you to shepherd as well as command."

Admiral Rowley changed tack again, "It is said that Commander Powell does not hold you in esteem. Will this create difficulty?"

Donland smiled, "I would say not. We have served together and as I reported, he commanded *Medusa* after Captain Okes went down. He is a fine seaman and a fine officer."

"Commander, what I need to know is will he follow your orders?"

Donland did not hesitate, "Aye, he will, I have no doubts and every confidence in him."

Admiral Rowley was satisfied; he nodded. "Tomorrow, the three of you report to me at ten."

"Aye Sir," Donland answered. In the hall he considered what he had told Admiral Rowley concerning Powell. He did have every confidence in the man, whether Powell still held hard feelings and envy, he did not know. It was possible that Powell was still angry but he was not willing to let such interfere with his duty. He was pleased to learn that Powell had received his step and a command of his own.

He was not taken aback that there were some in the fleet

that dared speak aloud their doubts of his loyalty. It did, however, concern him that those doubts would reach Rowley's ears. Jealousy was an evil all unto its own. But such was customary in the midshipmen's mess and the wardroom of any ship. Higher command appeared to be no different.

Asa Little and Honest John were waiting at the quay with the gig. Honest was now his coxs'n, which was David's suggestion so Donland felt obligated. The boy wasn't alone in his sorrow and was it not for David's suggestion he'd have no coxs'n.

He set aside those thoughts for the matters of the present. The loading and transporting troops would be of little consequence providing there were not too many of them. The munitions and stores for a sizeable force would tax the speed of each sloop and dictate where they could sail. These were concerns he could not address until he knew the numbers. Weather was an unstated element not addressed. February in the Carolinas could either be mild or brutal, changeable from one day to the next. He would set Jackson to inspecting the men's kits to ensure they were prepared for either climate.

Lyons words came to him, "Do not go blindly trusting those who command." And what was it, something to the effect, "They do not care for your suffering only their success." He decided that Admiral Rowley would not be beyond looking to his own success at the expense of the suffering others would endure. The delivery of troops and munitions to a hostile shore is far easier to plan than to execute.

The gig bumped alongside *Hornet.* Honest rose to assist Donland to the ladder. The side party came to attention. Donland doffed his hat.

"Orders Captain?" Jackson asked.

"Not as yet Mister Jackson," he answered and stepped close to speak that others would not overhear. "Inspect the men's kits for we may endure cold weather. I would that they have what they need before orders come to us." Then in a normal voice, "I will be in my cabin, send Mister Aldridge to me."

Aldridge appeared before Donland had his coat off. The heat in the cabin even with the skylight open was like a baker's oven. A little cold weather would not be a discomfort.

"Go to the Three Roses Inn, you will find it opposite of the church on the square. Secure a room for a party of six. After you have done that, take my compliments to Captain Powell of *Stinger* and to Captain Newland of *Jacket*. They are to dine with me tonight at seven at the inn and each is to bring one of their lieutenants. Tell them orders are forthcoming."

"Aye Sir!" Aldridge answered and turned to leave.

"Mister Aldridge!" Donland called, "A change of clothing would be in order before you go."

Aldridge looked down at his soiled breeches and dirty shirt. "Aye Sir," he replied and set off.

Two hours later, a knock at the cabin door drew Donland's attention from the chart he had just picked up. "Enter!" he said without looking up.

"Captain Donland," Sumerford said.

He looked up at that. "Mathias! I thought I'd seen the last of you."

"Not yet, not yet and not for some time."

"Sit and tell. A glass of wine?" Donland offered.

"Water if you please and lots of it. Damnable hot, eh?"

"Aye," Donland said as he rounded the table to sit in the chair beside Sumerford.

No sooner had he sat than Honest appeared with a jug

of water. He then produced two glasses and poured.

"Thank you Honest," Donland said.

Sumerford took the glass Honest offered. He said nothing but drank the glass in three gulps and held it out to be filled again. Once filled, he held it and said, "I've a letter from Cousin Betty, dated November, no mention of you. Just of the balls she has attended in Charleston and those who she'd met that I might know."

Donland considered Sumerford's words. The letter was almost three months getting to him. She may have met someone to fall in love with. He put the thought from his mind as quickly as it had come.

"Surely you've not come just to tell me that," Donland said.

"No, on the contrary. Wanted to let you know that you will have the joy of my company on your cruise," Sumerford smiled then drank.

"As a trader or as an agent?" Donland asked.

"I'll only say as a passenger until we reach our destination."

"I will enjoy your companionship. You will have Mister Jackson's quarters."

"Nay, I am displeased to tell you that you will need his quarters. You will have another guest that you will be delighted to extend your warmest hospitality to. Sorry, but I am not at liberty to name him at this time."

"Ever the agent," Donland grinned and said. He sipped from his glass and said, "Forewarned is fore armed."

"True, true. And, by the way I will dine with you this evening."

Donland managed," My apologies, I can't attend you tonight as I am otherwise engaged."

"Three Roses Inn at seven with Captains Powell and Newland," Sumerford said with a hint of humor. "I was at the inn while your young officer was making the arrangements."

"You will be joining us?" Donland asked.

"If you will have me?"

"Appears I have no recourse. Perhaps with an ample supply of cheap wine your tongue will loosen and I shall come away the better."

"I think not, others much easier on the eyes than you have tried that route with no success."

"I've no doubt of that." Donland said and grinned broadly.

Sumerford, Donland and Andrews arrived at the inn to find Powell and Newland waiting. Powell's greeting was pleasant but reserved.

Donland introduced Sumerford and Andrews. Powell followed with his introduction of his lieutenant Tomberlin, a square-jawed stump of a man with red hair and Newland introduced his; a large beefy black-haired man named Miller. All present appeared years older than Donland. As he considered those gathered at the table, all were at least thirty save himself and Andrews. He would do well to remember this in the future. And, remember they are not his equals as he is senior in rank and they subordinate to him.

Sumerford must have sensed the unease. "Either in their wisdom or their foolishness the powers that be are putting us under Captain Donland's orders," he said as he lifted his glass. "To Captain Donland!"

Each face seemed to hold a measure of surprise but they lifted their glasses. Donland noted that Miller grimaced.

Newland asked, "Where are we bound?"

Before Donland could answer Sumerford said, "That you will learn tomorrow from Admiral Rowley. He requires your presence at ten. You will have opportunity to ask your questions then. But for now, let us drink, lie and get drunk!"

Donland was relieved. He lifted his glass and drank, as

did each of the others.

Well into the meal and the wine, Tomberlin remarked, "Captain Donland has done well on this station."

Each man understood the reference was to prize money.

"Aye," Miller said with a hint of disdain. "He'll make us all rich if not dead."

Donland and the others let the remark pass.

Miller stared hard at Donland and said. "Bloody admirals toss the prime cuts to the favorites and the rest have to take the leavings."

No one replied, and all pretended not to hear. It was well known that Newland had served under Admiral Rowley as a midshipman. It was widely speculated that familiarity and favoritism landed Newland his step and command of *Jacket.*

"Captain Powell what of *Medusa*?" Donland asked to move the conversation in another direction.

"Bound for England two weeks ago. Captain Pettibone has temporary command for the passage."

"England, the thought of it makes me shiver and my bones ache," Newland lamented.

"Ah, the ladies that need warming," Andrews said.

"And bedding is what you meant to say," added Tomberlin.

"Aye, that too, that too," Andrews said beaming.

"To England!" Sumerford said and lifted his glass for a toast.

On this day there were two lieutenants seated on the benches of the house with blue shutters, each to his own bench. Donland did not know either man. The clerk sitting behind his small desk was unchanged from the day before.

"Your name sir?" The man asked as Donland removed his hat.

Jacket. Each is to be loaded equally. We will also be caring a company of soldiers, at least a hundred men and I want them equally distributed as well. They will have their kits and are to keep their kits with them. We've not space in the holds for anything other than the war materials we are to transport. Let no man bring more than his kit aboard. Understood?"

"Aye Captain," Jones said and asked, "but what if the other captains object?"

"Mister Jones they will not and to ensure you have no difficulty Mister Jackson will be by your side. Now you best be about the task."

"But . . . "Jones managed," and that was all he got out before Donland said, "Be about it Mister Jones!"

"Aye Sir," Jones said and left the cabin mumbling.

Donland was on deck through the loading of *Hornet*, which was completed, in late afternoon. He had decided not to bring the soldiers onboard until all three sloops were loaded with stores and munitions and ready to stand out to sea.

Jacket came next. Donland went aboard.

Pipes tweeted and the side party was smartly turned out.

Donland observed the formalities but in Newland's cabin he stated the obvious, "Commander Newland I will be coming aboard throughout the evening and honors are not necessary. We have too much to accomplish in too little time. Lieutenant Jackson and Mister Jones will assist Lieutenant Miller with the loading of your ship.

"Aye Sir," Newland answered with relief evident in his voice.

Donland said, "Let us go below to your cabin."

The cabin contained a sea chest, two three-legged stools and a table strewn with charts. There were no chairs.

"I've not had opportunity to purchase chairs." Newland apologized.

"Applewhite bring us some rum if you please." Newland

called to his coxs'n.

"Aye Captain," the man answered from beyond the bulkhead.

"How many men have you aboard?" Donland asked.

"Sixty-one Sir, not counting the officers and supernumeraries. I've not had much luck in gaining more men. The prime seaman are all taken and only the crippled and drunks remain."

Donland stared out the stern windows and said without looking at Newland, "The captains of the ships that were ordered to send men would have sent the dregs of their companies. Even your officers and midshipmen are those unlikely to be missed."

"Aye," Newland said.

The tone of unease was there. Donland heard it clearly and said. "Your first seems a capable man."

"Aye, good with sail handling and navigation," Newland stated.

Donland asked, "Difficult?"

Newland was guarded. "On occasion but I've not gotten to know the man well."

"What about your other lieutenant?"

Newland smiled and managed, "Acting only, he's not sat for the board. Johnson is competent but not very firm with the company as yet."

"Benjamin," Donland said using Newland's given name, "We've a task that will require the best of our ships and our companies. As with the shifting of stores and cargoes to achieve a vessel's best sailing qualities we shall have to do so with the men we are allotted. If we are to succeed in this endeavor we must not allow slackers, mischief-makers or sea lawyers to hold sway over even a few men. Keep a watchful eye."

Newland answered with wariness in his voice, "Aye."

Applewhite came in carrying a pewter tray and placed it carefully atop the charts.

"Thank you Applewhite, I'll pour," Newland said dismissing the man.

Donland took the offered cup that was half-filled with grog. "To you and *Jacket*," he toasted.

"To you Sir," Newland replied.

They drank. The grog was more water than rum.

Newland winced.

"Not very good is it?" Donland asked with a grin.

Newland composed himself. "It's all I have. I spent all my money at the chandlers to be able to get *Jacket* to sea. Bloodsuckers!"

Donland sighed. "Aye, but I would venture more like sharks smelling blood in the water. I can say with confidence that you are not the first nor will you be the last they will fleece. You're not to be faulted but a bit of advice; in the future have your first lieutenant or your sailing master accompany you when you must deal with them."

"Aye, I'll heed your advice," Newland said.

"A firm hand Mister Newland, and a wary eye. Show your men that you trust them to do their duty and they will do it." Donland said as he turned to go.

Newland did not reply.

"Let us see to the loading," Donland said.

Newland seemed to linger. He was slow to set the cup down and follow.

"Something troubling you Benjamin?" Donland asked.

"Aye Sir," Newland said firmly.

They eyes met for only an instant and Newland looked down.

"Confidence Benjamin? Is that it? You question if I have confidence in you?"

Newland met Donland's eyes and was about to speak but Donland held up a hand and took a step closer. They were within arm's reach of one another.

Donland said in a low but firm voice, "You are the captain of this vessel, a king's officer. Admiral Rowley tasked you to command so what I think or what others think is of no consequence. Do your duty and none will find fault, for I shall not."

Donland stood in the bow of *Jacket* watching the loading; Newland was aft. There were storms ahead, of this Donland was certain. Newland was a competent man, had shown himself to be as the provost. But beyond what he had observed of the incident with Dr. Fredricks he did not know. Miller's jealousy was evident but it fell to Newland as captain to assert his authority over the company including Miller. He did not envy the man the task for Miller was a hard man and coupled with his physical stature could be intimidating. The two of them would have to sort out their differences it was not his place to interfere unless there was mutiny.

Jackson and Jones worked well together. Net after net was swayed up and deposited into the holds of *Jacket*. Newland, Donland observed, had left the quarterdeck and was in the thick of the loading and stowing. It was work that should have been delegated to Miller. But Donland could not interfere, Newland would have to learn and the only way was by making mistakes.

Jackson wiped the sweat from his face with a rag. He said something to Jones and started toward Donland who stood in the shade across from the quay.

"That's the last of it for *Jacket*. She'll have room for the troops."

"That the lot for *Stinger*?" Donland asked pointing to what remained on the quay.

"Aye Captain, about the same as what we put aboard *Hornet*. Mister Jones did the parceling out and I stayed to his numbers."

"Good work Mister Jackson." Donland replied.

"What about the troops?" Jackson asked.

Donland pulled his watch from his pocket. "Quarter after seven," he said and continued, "The army should be arriving within the hour. I've instructed *Hornet* and *Jacket* to send their boats ashore at eight and to begin ferrying the troops. Mister Andrews will see to them on *Hornet* and Captain Newland will shift as needed I'm sure."

A clatter of hooves on cobblestones caused both Donland and Jackson to look up. Two officers in redcoats trotted two large brown horses toward the quay. They reigned up near where Jones was leaning on a stack of crates.

"You there! Where is the officer in charge here?" The army officer snarled.

"Captain Donland, over there!" Jones answered and pointed in Donland's direction.

The officer wheeled his horse toward Donland. "Where's the bloody ships?" he asked in a huff.

Donland stepped from the shade. "Captain Donland of *Hornet*." Donland stated. "It is my good pleasure to make your acquaintance Major Ellington.

"Well Sir, where are the ships. My company will be arriving shortly."

Jacket had slipped the mooring and her sails were being unfurled. Several men were fending her off the quay with long boat-hooks.

"That is *Jacket*," Donland said as he pointed. "She will be sending her boats back to ferry your men out to her. *Hornet*, is sending her boats as we speak. We've yet to put stores and munitions aboard *Stinger* but once we have we will ferry your men to her."

"By gawd, Sir they're rowboats!" Major Ellington exclaimed.

"We have room, sir. Thirty-three men to a ship and a quick passage; far faster than a troopship."

Ellington was about to speak but the other officer said,

"We were given to understand there would be frigates."

Donland almost smiled. The officer was attempting to put things into a proper perspective before Ellington could bluster. He followed suit, "Admiral Rowley deemed the sloops would be faster and able to carry your men across the shallows where frigates could not go. Less danger to enemy fire."

"Just so, just so," the officer said.

" Pellew stop babbling!" Ellington snorted.

To Donland he said, "Rowley said there would be frigates."

Donland was firm. "Major Ellington there are no frigates. My orders are to transport your men, the stores and the munitions. I will begin ferrying your men as soon as they arrive. If you please, have them sorted out into thirds. You will go aboard *Stinger* and Captain Pellew will go aboard *Jacket*. One of your other officers will go aboard *Hornet*. We've little time left to us so let us be about it!"

"Our horses…" Major Ellington said but got no further.

"There's no room for horses Major Ellington," Donland stated.

"Gentlemen, gentlemen. Maybe I can assist," A man dressed in civilian clothes said. He looked like a merchant. Ellington and Pellew looked down at him and dislike was on their face.

"I'm Captain Furman and am tasked to be your liaison. I can assure you that there will be suitable mounts for your officers once we arrive."

Donland was glad for Furman's intervention. "My compliments Captain Furman, your arrival is timely."

"Seems so Captain," Furman replied.

He then looked up at Major Ellington. "Captain Donland has explained the logistics to you Sir, let this be an end to squabbling. Mister Jennings will see to your horses and as I said, others will be provided at our destination."

Captain Pellew dismounted and reached for the bridle of

Ellington's horse. Two files of soldiers rounded the corner of a building at that same moment. "The company," Pellew said.

Ellington glanced back and said, "About bloody time." He dismounted.

Donland crossed the road back to the quay. *Jacket* was well away and *Stinger*, under sweeps, was approaching the quay. Jackson was enjoying a drink of water and some sort of red fruit.

"Hot work," Donland said as he came near.

"Aye Captain. Hot work and I'll be glad to be aboard," Jackson remarked.

"Your lieutenant?" A voice behind Donland asked.

He turned to find Captain Furman had followed.

"Aye, this is Lieutenant Jackson, first officer of *Hornet*."

To Jackson he said, "This is Captain Furman, he will be sailing with us."

Furman and Jackson eyed each other for a moment and then Furman thrust out his hand and said, "Captain Donland I have two men who will be joining us before we sail. I trust you have room for them?"

"Aye, they will share your cabin," Donland answered.

Stinger made fast to the quay and Powell came off followed by Lieutenant Tomberlin.

Donland introduced Captain Furman and got to the business at hand.

"Captain Powell if I may with your compliments task Mister Tomberlin with supervising the ferrying of the soldiers. Mister Jackson will see to the loading of *Stinger* as he has the other two sloops."

"Aye Sir," Powell agreed.

Tomberlin half-turned and stared at the troops.

"Mister Tomberlin," Donland raised his voice to gain the man's attention, "Major Ellington is in command and Captain Pellew is his second. Pellew will be of great help to you."

Tomberlin turned back to face Donland but did not reply. The smile that followed along with a nod of his head left no doubt that he understood the difficulty he was to face.

After a second nod of his head he managed, "Captain Pellew, yes, a man of my temperament."

"Captain Furman when will your men arrive?" Donland inquired.

"They are here already sir."

"Very good then, you and your men will go across to *Hornet* on the boat tying up to the quay now. Mister Aldridge will see to your needs." Donland said and pointed to the boat.

"Thank you, Captain Donland your hospitality is appreciated," Furman replied.

"Captain Donland may I offer you a refreshment?" Powell asked.

"Aye, it would come most welcome."

In stark contrast to Newland's cabin, Powell's was furnished with a maple desk, matching chairs with leather seat and arms. On the wall were seascape paintings. The deck was graced with a tapestry of yellow and green depicting a summer meadow.

"Wine or a liqueur?" Powell asked.

"Water if you please. I've eaten little today and either would be wasted," Donland answered.

A young man with light skin entered wearing black clothing. Donland's impression was that of an oriental.

"Water if you please Jaha," Powell requested.

Donland's attention wandered to a painting of coastline that appeared to be New England, perhaps upper New York.

"I don't know what that coast that is," Powell said. "The paintings, these furnishing, and Jaha came to me when we came upon pirates attacking a French merchantman. The pirates escaped, the merchantman sank. What you see is some of what we managed to take off. The remainder I sold and divided the proceeds among my crew."

"Fortunate for you and them," Donland said with admiration.

"Aye but the real treasure was the eight seaman I signed into the muster book. None of them were French and all are Jaha's kinsmen. They were more than grateful for their rescue."

Jaha returned bearing a silver tray laden with a glass pitcher filled with water, two glass goblets, a silver bowl of sliced lemons, a small silver bowl of fine white sugar and a covered silver slaver. He placed the tray on a lace-covered sideboard.

Jaha poured water into the two glasses then uncovered the slaver. Cheeses and breads surrounded slivers of meat, both dark and light.

Powell grinned and said, "thank you Jaha, we shall manage."

"Captain Donland may I serve you or do you prefer to serve yourself?"

Donland smiled; his mouth watered. "Thank you James, I will manage."

They both squeezed lemon into the glasses and using a silver spoon added several heaping spoonfuls of sugar. The result was better than any wine Donland had ever tasted.

Powell set his half-empty glass on the table. "Sir," He began, "I am the one that is thankful. I appreciate the kindness you've shown me," he managed haltingly.

"Kindness? What kindness?" Donland asked.

"*Stinger* Sir, I'd not have her were it not for your kindness."

"James, you were my senior, let us set aside formability and speak as friend to friend. Call me Isaac here. The kindness to which to refer, you more than earned, as first on *Medusa* and then when commanding her in the fight with the Spanish frigate. The admiral saw your merit."

"So you say Isaac, but it is told about that you sent letters and had words with the admiral on my behalf. But for those I would still be first on *Medusa*."

Donland was at a loss for words. He had not supposed others would know of his boldness with Admiral Rowley. The Admiral had chosen another from his flagship for *Stinger* and Donland risked his career to put forth Powell. In the end, the admiral had seen the merit of Powell's promotion.

Donland remembered Rowley's words and dared not share them with Powell. Rowley had said, "In the future Mister Donland, do not be so modest in your reports and do not presume I will tolerate your interference."

He gave a slight shake of his head at the memory. "Let us not speak more of this James. You have earned your step, probably more so than I have."

"Not so Isaac, there are those in English Harbor that are jealous of your success but there are none that would argue that you did not earn your step. I am in your debt and offer my hand in friendship and service to your command."

Donland took his hand. "I too offer my friendship. Now let us be about the king's business."

Chapter Five

Hornet catted her anchor at two bells in the morning watch. Donland ordered *make sail* to be hoisted, and they were away. Her deck was crowded with the thirty soldiers and *Hornet's* crew for the most part, held their tongues as they went about their duties.

The gray of the morning quickly gave way to bright blue sky. The wind was fresh and soon rid *Hornet's* deck of the stench of unwashed bodies. The sails were hard with the press of wind and *Hornet's* bow cut through troughs and waves pushing a fine bow wave as she did so.

Donland studied the two sloops trailing. *Stinger's* press of sail matched *Hornet's* but *Jacket* seemed slower and her sails were ill trimmed. Even from the distance that separated the two ships Donland's sharp eyes saw a slight slacking as wind was spilled. He would do nothing for now. Newland would have to sort his company out and Miller would have to be more attentive to his duty.

By midday the soldiers were complaining of heat and sun. They sought the shade of the sails and were ordered by their sergeants and corporals to remain in ranks along the gunnels. Donland had made the point that the men were to be in two divisions one to larboard and one to starboard. He could not have them underfoot while men attended to sail and rigging.

Jacket was well off the pace and the distance between her and *Stinger* was more than double than between *Hornet* and *Stinger.*

"Mister Welles make *Jacket's* number if you please. Send up, *make more sail,*" Donland ordered.

He had put off sending the signal for as long as he could.

"Acknowledged Captain," David reported after seeing the signal from *Jacket.*

"Mister Jackson take in a reef if you please," he ordered.

Powell would maintain the distance without having to be told.

Jacket's inability to keep pace was a growing concern. An encounter with the French or the Spanish or even an American privateer could be disastrous. Together they could fight clear of any frigate and sloops their size would keep their distance. But, *Jacket* sailing at a distance would be a tempting target.

At the turn of the glass *Jacket* had closed the distance only slightly. She was as slow as a troop transport. It would not do, not do at all.

"Mister Jackson reduce sail. We shall keep steerage way!" Donland ordered.

"Aye Captain," Jackson answered.

"Mister Welles make *Stinger's* number if you please. Send up, come alongside.

"Aye Captain," David replied and began to bend on the signal.

Stinger was soon up to *Hornet* and the two sloops waited

for their companion. Great humps of cloud could be seen in the west near the horizon. The afternoon would be filled with squalls. Donland did not want to be caught lying-to again. He would have to discover Newland's difficulty.

"Mister Dewitt what do you make of the weather?" Donland asked.

"Squalls Captain, more'n one blow I'd say."

Donland had decided.

"Mister Jackson a word if you please," he called to Jackson who was standing starboard clutching the main shrouds in one hand.

Donland would not have to tell Powell his concern. The man was an experienced officer and would be sharing Donland's concern for *Jacket*. He would probably be wondering what was to be done.

"Mister Jackson I shall go aboard *Jacket*. You will command here until I return at nightfall. We will have squalls but none that should be bothersome. Tack as you deem necessary and *Stinger* and *Jacket* will follow. Mister Dewitt has our course."

"Aye Sir," Jackson replied.

Donland went below for his sword and a pistol. Sumerford seemed to be waiting for him.

"You may require assistance commodore," Sumerford stated.

"Commodore?" Donland was taken aback.

"That's what they call the one who commands a squadron if I am correct."

"True Matthias but this is hardly a squadron. Three sloops commanded by three lieutenants is hardly worth consideration by their lordships."

Sumerford was grinning. He put an arm on Donland's shoulder and said. "I shall accompany you commodore. Every commodore needs a servant to do the dirty work and I am very practiced at dirty work."

Donland surmised that Sumerford's grinning face did not

match his words. Perhaps he knew something of Newland's company that may require closer scrutiny.

"Your sword should be a comfort to you," Sumerford said as he removed his hand.

"Aye, as well as your presence."

"That too, that too Isaac. A friend at your back is better than an unknown enemy at your front."

Hornet with *Stinger* keeping station on the larboard quarter waited a little more than an hour for *Jacket* to draw within hailing distance. For some unknown reason Newland had reduced sail well before reaching them. Something was clearly amiss. Donland was determined to know what it was before the day ended.

Newland's side-party piped Donland aboard. All appeared as it should be except for Newland's absence. Donland was wary. His quick examination of the deck proved his caution was not without merit. There were weapons where there should have been none. The soldiers appeared timid, they had no muskets and Captain Pellew was absent.

The word that came to Donland's mind was mutiny. The signs were all too in evidence. He would tread lightly until a course of action was required.

Sumerford said loudly to Donland, "The motion of that boat has made me a bit unwell. I shall go below and lie down," he did not wait for a reply or an escort but bolted for the hatchway with his hand over his mouth.

A bald man with burly arms and a large gut hurried after Sumerford.

Donland placed his hand on the hilt of his sword. He turned slightly and saw that *Hornet* was getting under way and spreading her canvas. *Stinger* was following suit.

Donland gauged the situation and said loudly, "Mister Miller I shall go below, there are some details about the landing I need to discuss with Captain Newland."

Miller said nothing and did not move.

Donland was keenly aware of the eyes on him as he descended the hatch followed by Honest. He was pleased to see Sumerford waiting just beyond the hatch. The bald man lay at his feet. Six others sat on the deck staring at the pistol Sumerford was pointing at them.

"He slipped and hit his head," Sumerford said with a straight face.

Donland hurried past him to the cabin that was guarded by two marines. They stood aside as he reached for the door.

"Honest assist Mister Sumerford while I attend Captain Newland," Donland ordered.

"Aye Captain," Honest answered and pulled his knife.

Newland lay in his bed fully dressed. He was not bound and his eyes were wide open.

"Where's Captain Pellew?" Donland asked in a hushed voice.

Newland did not answer.

"Mutiny?" Donland whispered.

Newland did not answer. His eyes were glazed. He was sweating.

"Speak man. What is happening here?" Donland insisted.

Newland made to answer but it was as if the man could not get his lips to move.

Donland did not know what ailed Newland but it was clear the man was not capable of commanding the ship. He would have to go on deck and brace Miller. He turned to go.

"Drugged!" Sumerford said." He's not sick, not drunk, I've seen it before."

"Are you certain?" Donland asked.

"Yes I'm certain. Either by his own hand or another's but drugged none the less."

"I shall go on deck and brace Miller. You stay and see if you get bring Captain Newland from his stupor."

Newland's hand reached out and grasped Donland's

sleeve.

In a weak voice, barely audible, Newland said. "The man is the devil, and the company is afraid of him and his bullyboys. There was naught I could do."

"Aye, I feared as much," Donland said. "I do not fault you."

He turned away from Newland, "Mister Sumerford I shall require your assistance to set things to rights," Donland said in a normal voice.

Sumerford opened his coat revealing three small Queen Anne pistols similar to the one he was holding.

"Let us be about it then," Donland said.

Sumerford reached out and caught Donland's arm. He whispered, "I will go up the other hatch and if you are threatened, I will be able to divert their attention."

Donland whispered, "I shall give you time."

"Honest you go with him. Two should be better than one for this work," Donland said to his coxs'n. "But first let us deal with these."

He pulled a shirt from a peg and began to rip it into strips and tossed a handful to Honest and then some to Sumerford. "Bind their hands and gag them."

Honest did as he was told while Donland held the pistol.

"You men," Donland addressed them." Up the hatch and no tricks or I'll put a ball in you!"

The men were hesitant until Donland drew his sword and prodded the first man. "Now!" He shouted.

They started for the hatch. Each gave a wary a look over a shoulder.

"I will send these up and then follow. It should give you enough time to reach the other hatch. Honest watch Mister Sumerford's back while I send this lot up."

"Aye Captain," Honest said.

Sumerford and Honest hurried away toward the bow.

Miller and four men stood only a few paces from the hatch, in their hands were swords and pistols.

"Take his weapons!" Miller ordered.

"Try and one of you will die, who will it be?" Donland asked.

The men hesitated as Donland pointed the pistol to each man in turn.

He said loud enough for all to hear, "Give up Miller, this is a fight you can't win. You've committed no hanging offense as yet. Neither have you men. But if you persist each of you shall surely hang before sunset. Look there, *Hornet* has come up into the wind and she is tacking as we speak. *Stinger* is following her round," Donland said and nodded in *Hornet's* direction.

Miller and the four men turned and looked. The four studied the tacking ships.

Beyond the men Donland caught movement, a man wearing a straw hat, no shoes or shirt shouldered a mop. He carried a bucket in his other hand. The man seemed oblivious to the drama unfolding before him.

Suddenly, Miller wheeled about while raising his pistol.

He shouted, "they'll not fire nor come aboard as long as I have you!"

The others turned about and began to ready their weapons to strike.

The mop handle struck Miller such a blow as to send him sprawling into Donland's arms. The barrel of Donland's pistol broke bone as it came down on Miller's arm.

Sumerford shouted a warning to the others, "One move lads and it will be your last." He held a pistol in each hand.

Donland was not surprised to see that the man with the mop was Honest. He grinned.

Sumerford was as full of tricks as the king's jester. In Honest he had found a willing accomplice.

"Drop your weapons!" Donland commanded.

The four men did as ordered. Miller made no move to

rise or reach for a weapon. He was out cold and a gash at the back of his head spurt blood onto the deck.

"That was well Done Mister Sumerford," Donland said.

Miller began to stir.

"Get him on his feet," Donland said and pointed the pistol at one of the men.

Miller with the assistance of the man regained his feet. He was hunched over. One hand went to the back of his head. He drew it away and studied the blood on his hand. His knees buckled, and he went down to one knee. The man assisting him bent to help Miller to his feet.

A glint of metal flashed and Miller stood quickly. In his hand was a small knife, he lunged quickly at Donland.

The pistol in Donland's hand barked, and he felt the buck of it. The ball tore into Miller's stomach. At that same moment there was another flash of metal as Honest buried his knife in Miller's back.

"Ugh!" Escaped from Miller's lips as blood erupted from his mouth. He went down, lifeless.

"Bastard!" Honest shouted at the dead man as he pulled his knife free.

Hornet and *Stinger* came alongside.

"Do you need assistance?" Jackson bellowed across the distance.

"No!" Donland shouted back. "Keep station!"

Sumerford had gone below and was with Captain Newland. It took the better part of an hour before, under Sumerford's administrations, for Newland to become coherent.

"Drugged you say?" Newland said weakly.

"Aye," Donland answered. "Miller couldn't kill you for that would see him hanged. But if you were unfit for command, he would have a free hand."

Newland held his head in his hands and did not look at Donland.

Sumerford smiled and said. "He'll mend in a few days. No more than a hangover."

Donland considered Sumerford's words. "A hangover, eh, very fortunate considering the events."

Resolved he said, "Captain Newland I shall rejoin *Hornet. Jacket* is your ship and these are your men. Sort it out, we've delayed long enough. I will send another officer across to assist you."

Newland looked up. "Aye Sir," he replied and braced his hands on the table and pushed himself up. Johnson, the acting lieutenant steadied his captain.

Donland placed a hand on Newland's shoulder. "It was a near thing. You'd have died in a few days. I'd not known the cause and mourned your loss," he smiled, "I'd not want to lose you."

"Mister Johnson if you please, assist Captain Newland onto the deck," Donland said to the young man.

On deck Sumerford asked, "What happens to this lot?"

Donland looked out to sea and said, "Hanging if Captain Newland is to remain in command."

"Bad as that?"

"Aye," Donland answered.

After a moment he added, "Of course for our part there will be reports to be written. I will need a statement from you for mine. Captain Newland will write his own and there shall be an inquiry. The death of an officer will not go unnoticed by the admiralty."

They stood gazing out to sea. Behind them Newland, with his hands braced on the railing, was giving orders and men were obeying.

"Off your arses!" A voice Donland recognized as Captain Pellew's bellowed. He was followed by Honest.

"Sergeants form of your squads for inspections!" Pellew bellowed again.

"Isaac how did Mister Jackson know there was trouble and to come about?" Sumerford asked.

Donland faced him, "There are times when communication is not possible but necessary. We were under observation from the moment that we stepped aboard *Jacket.* It is customary for a visiting officer to doff his hat. If you recall, I did not."

"A signal!" Sumerford said with understanding.

"Aye."

"Captain!" David called.

Donland turned first to David and then in the direction the boy pointed. He took a glass from the rack and focused it. A body hung from the mainmast yardarm of *Jacket.* It was followed by a second. He watched for another minute but there was not a third.

"Justice," Dewitt said softly.

"Aye," Donland answered. He only hoped that Newland had made the correct decision to hang two men instead of four. The crack on the back of the head with the mop handle had not killed Miller. And, were it not for being shot and knifed he would be one of those hanging from the yard. His death was no loss to the ship. But it did leave Newland without a second in command.

Andrews accepted being acting first lieutenant aboard *Jacket* with eagerness. He was the logical choice to aid Newland although young but he was steady in all respects. Newland appeared to accept the appointment with grace. Young Johnson seemed to pout. It could not be helped for Newland needed an experienced man.

Andrews' going across to *Jacket* was a loss, one that Donland hoped he would not regret in the future. But their task of delivering the soldiers and the munitions meant that all three ships had to rely upon one another. Andrews would be a stabilizing influence for *Jacket* for all aboard her would know that although his captain was aboard *Hornet*, he would protect one of his own.

The afternoon squalls broke upon *Hornet*. The soldiers cheered, and the seaman ignored them. *Jacket* was holding station on *Hornet*'s quarter as *Stinger* brought up the rear. Donland thought to himself of how the squalls of weather were easier to endure than the squalls brought about by men. It was as Admiral Rowley had said, "You will have to shepherd them as much as command them."

At dawn *Jacket* was on station behind *Hornet* as she was to be for the remainder of the voyage. The bodies had been removed from her yardarm. Donland observed the ship's sails were taut and her company was about their tasks.

"A beautiful sight are they not?" Sumerford said referencing *Jacket* and *Stinger* under sail. Both heeled to the wind exactly the same and both with a white surging bow wave. Their sails bellowing against the bright blue sky.

Donland lowered the telescope. "Aye."

"Your man Andrews seemed to have put some backbone in that lot," Sumerford added.

"Aye, he had a good teacher in Mister Jackson." Donland said giving credit where he knew it belonged.

Sumerford mused, "At first I thought your choice to send the young man was in error but I see it for what it is. Jackson is your right hand, and you'd be crippled without him so you sent Andrews. Which, in hindsight was needful for him and them. The young bird tests his wings."

"Aye Mathias, aye. We all have to do it at sometime."

Donland thought of *Morgador* and how unsure of himself he had been when he stepped aboard to deliver her to Antigua. It had been a lofty step to command a frigate with the prize crew, even if only for a few days. Yet it had fallen to him and not to Powell because Captain Okes needed Powell.

Had Okes decided otherwise their roles might well be reversed but as fate had so destined, they each had their step and command.

Chapter Six

Weak sunlight seeped through a gray layer of cloud. The piercing cold reminded Donland of New Haven some nine hundred miles north of Port Royal. *Hornet* lay anchored alongside *Stinger* and *Jacket.*

Cold wind blew through the rigging. The skylight overhead in Donland's cabin was closed to retain as much warmth as possible. On the table sat the remains of the pork roast they had been covered in onions and garlic. Jackson, Dewitt, Captain Furman, Donland and Sumerford had eaten their fill and sopped the juices with ship's biscuits.

"Snow before nightfall," Dewitt observed.

Jackson replied from across the table, "I hope you are wrong. Snow and cold are a torment to my old bones."

"Snow or no snow," Donland said, "we will bear up until we have off-loaded every solider and every cask and every barrel."

"Captain where are the wagons bound once loaded?" Dewitt asked.

Donland studied Sumerford's face and answered. "That I have not been privileged to know. Our orders are to enter the roads and off-load everything we have been entrusted with. Where it is taken and who takes it is not in our orders or our concern"

"Captain," Sumerford began, "your task may not be complete with the off-loading. There are wagons to be loaded, and the goods transported north to a ferry. The soldiers are here to ensure the wagons make it to the ferry. Should there be need, your ships and your men will assist. Captain Furman is to accompany the wagons to their final destination."

Donland was keenly aware of what Sumerford wasn't saying. A force of several hundred men would only *assist* if there were an equal or larger number of enemies about. He chose to keep silent.

Jackson was the bull in the china shop. "So you want us to fight all the way to the ferry just to get those wagons away?"

Sumerford looked first to Donland then leaned back in his chair. "Mister Jackson your observation is correct. If we encounter sufficient force to warrant assistance, Captain Donland will do so."

From his pocket, Sumerford fished a small black-as-tar cigar and lit it. He continued. "We have arrived at our destination so you should know the purpose we are about. Our mission is urgent, the munitions are for Colonel James Boyd who is to raise as many men as possible to fight against the colonials. His intent is to defeat the militias in the Carolinas and Georgia and gather sufficient force to move on to Virginia. Sir Henry Clinton has encouraged Boyd and lent his support. The arms in the holds of the sloops were sent from England to meet Boyd's needs."

Jackson, "A fool's errand!" Jackson said bluntly.

"And you know this to be true?" Sumerford asked.

"Aye," Jackson said. "Those here about want nothing to do with England or the crown. I've lived among these people, I know them and Boyd will be lucky to find a hundred for his cause."

"True!" Dewitt added. "The army had been savage in their dealings with the colonists. Houses and barns burned, livestock confiscated, boys pressed into service and women raped. Such atrocities only harden the resolve of these folk to end British rule."

Sumerford appeared amused. Donland was not.

"We will do our duty as ordered. We will off-load the munitions and we will assist Captain Furman," Donland said. "Those are our orders."

Sumerford re-lit his cigar from the candle on the table. He puffed twice. "Boyd's representative is to arrive tomorrow or the next day. The plan was for the munitions to be at Land's End by the first of February. That has been achieved. It is now up to Captain Furman to make contact with Boyd's representative and attend to the details of unloading, packing and shipping."

"Snow you say Mister Dewitt?" Donland asked.

"Aye Captain, there will be snow," Dewitt answered.

Dawn came and Donland stood aft of the helm staring at the brown lifeless river shoreline. He was growing restless and worried for they had arrived as ordered. Even as he stood there, he had little doubt that riders on swift horses were riding to Charles Town with the news of their presence.

"Where are they?" He almost asked aloud. The longer Boyd's people delayed the greater the danger to his command.

Major Ellington was ashore with fifty of his men providing protection on the larboard side riverbank. Captain Pellew was on the starboard riverbank with thirty men. Pickets had been posted a quarter mile inland. They would have time to get to deeper water if a warning was given. He had to be content with their security and wait. But, he had decided to withdraw to deep water before nightfall. It was the prudent thing to do. What could be done had been done. He would wait until nightfall but no longer.

Ellington had asked for the two six pound cannons but Donland considered the risk too great. He doubted the admirals would be forgiving should those cannon fall into the hands of the colonials. Ellington had walked away in a huff.

"Signal from shore Sir!" David said as he was admitted to Donland's cabin. "They've a boat and coming across."

"Thank God!" Donland said much relieved. "Now we can be about this task. Tell Mister Aldridge to signal the other captains to come aboard."

"Aye Sir," David answered and hurried from the cabin.

The representative identified himself as Major Seviers. Five men accompanied him and were dressed in heavy civilian coats and clothing each sported a beard and mustache. The lot of them appeared to be farmers.

Donland greeted each man and invited him below. Honest had set out wine, glasses, cheeses and ship's biscuits.

Powell and Newland arrived together. There were not seats for ten men in the tiny cabin so all were standing elbow to elbow around the chart table. The newcomers smelled of horse, tobacco and whiskey. Considering the cold and their travels they were entitled to smell for no man would brave a bath.

Once the introductions were concluded, Seviers laid out what was to occur in the coming days. "We are to rendezvous with Colonel Boyd in Ninety-Six before the fifteen. He will have three thousand or more men by then and these arms and supplies must reach him before he moves on to Augusta to join Colonel Campbell. From there we will re-establish rule over Georgia and the Carolinas. Sir Henry Clinton has assured us of continued supplies and support."

Donland listened but was not concerned since the moving of the arms and supplies would be Seviers' mission and not his. He said, "We will begin unloading as soon as you are ready."

"I'm afraid it is not that simple Commander." Seviers said and tapped the chart on the table. "Here is Fort Lyttleton, we must subdue it so that we may advance without being molested."

Powell asked, "Do you have the troops to take the fort?"

Seviers looked up from the chart. "Sadly no, we must rely on your assistance. I had hoped Captain Furman would have more men with him but as he hasn't, we require all you can provide."

Powell looked to Donland as did the others in the cabin.

Donland straightened and said, "My orders are to assist Colonel Boyd's representatives in landing and preparing the transport of the munitions and supplies. The soldiers we have transported are to provide security during the landing of the munitions and supplies. There is no mention of capturing a fort nor of accompanying Colonel Boyd's representatives. However, I am certain the admiral would not be pleased should these munitions be captured and Colonel Boyd's representatives are captured. We shall therefore do as our orders state, assist and that means getting Captain Furman and these gentlemen well on their way to their rendezvous. Do you gentlemen agree?"

There was a chorus of, "Aye!"

He paused thoughtfully then continued, "Taking the fort is out of the question."

He looked to Seviers and asked, "Major Seviers do you have intelligence concerning the strength of the fort?"

"No more than thirty," Seviers stated.

Donland bent over the chart; time, distance and tide were his normal concerns not a military excursion on land. He made his decision.

"We can pin them in the fort while Captain Furman shepherds his charges through Port Royal and through Beauford. Taking the fort is not necessary and the loss of life to do so would be a waste. We shall send a force of two hundred with two six-pounders against the fort's defenders. I should think that sufficient to hold them at bay. Once Captain Furman is safely away, we shall withdraw. Is that agreeable Major Seviers?"

"Yes, I think that should do us well," Seviers answered.

Donland looked from man to man gauging their acceptance of the plan. "Captain Powell and Captain Newland you will each provide a six-pounder and thirty men. *Hornet* will supply the remaining men since we have almost a full company."

He turned to Seviers, "Are you familiar with the terrain around the fort? Can we find suitable cover for our men at a safe distance and force them to remain inside?"

Seviers reached into his coat and pulled out a folded hand-drawn map and laid it on top of the chart. "There's marshlands here and here," he said and pointed. "This is the road to the fort." He traced a line with his finger. "Along the road there are several groves of scrub pine and live oak. After dark we should be able to place our men without being seen."

"On the contrary Major Seviers, we want the men seen and we want them to see the cannon. They must think our intention is to attack. My concern is that we have cover and remain a safe distance."

Seviers studied his map and seemed to be recalling from memory the lay of the land. "Yes, I'm sure we can." He pointed to a spot on the map along the road. "Here is about as close as we can come, it's about a quarter-mile from the fort."

"It's settled then. Captain Powell and Captain Newland return to your commands. We will start landing the remaining soldiers and our men without delay. As to the munitions and supplies, those remaining aboard will see to unloading and loading for transport."

Sumerford knocked and entered unbidden. "It pays dividends to be wary of the adventurous," he said.

"How so?" Donland asked.

"A man who is willing to risk the lives of others will think nothing of yours."

"Are you speaking of Major Seviers?"

"Yes and no. You have yet to tell the brave Major Ellington of the plan. Betwixt the two majors a great deal of blood can flow. I shall do my best to mediate."

"Aye, see that you do." There was no humor in Donland's statement.

Donland's feet were like two blocks of ice. The cold wind with spitting snow seemed to cut right through his greatcoat. He wondered how the poorly dressed seamen were bearing the cold wearing thin trousers and jackets. They were hearty men but the change in climate would take its toll. But now, his attention was focused on leading these men to attack a fort.

"Bout a mile more," Seviers stated.

In front of them was a squad of red-coated soldiers and behind them marched the remainder of the company commanded by Major Ellington of Sussex. Following the soldiers were the seaman led by Lieutenant Jackson. The two six-pounders loaded on carts brought of the rear of the column.

Donland considered the leaden sky. More snow was in the offing if he was any judge of weather. They needed to hurry if his plan was to succeed. "Major Ellington! Quick march!" He shouted and set off at a trot."

He needed not look back for he heard Ellington's order and the jostle of men and equipment. Seviers was matching his stride and said, "They'll know we're a'coming."

"Aye, and that will serve us. They'll not want to venture out in this cold to face an unknown confident force."

Seviers replied, "I would not."

The squad of soldiers could be seen ahead standing in the road. Donland slowed, turned and waited for Major Ellington. "Form up your men and fire a volley."

"Yes Sir," Ellington replied and began calling out orders.

Jackson came lumbering to where Donland and Seviers were waiting as the soldiers filled in their ranks. "Have the men fall in behind the redcoats. Give a cheer."

"Aye Sir," Jackson said and hurried off with the seaman following.

"Major Seviers you go on ahead. I shall wait for the cannon to be brought up."

The ox carts bearing the cannon were slow. Donland waited, he was aware of the vapor of his breath. It would be cold during the night but he and his men would be able to warm themselves by campfires if they were delayed in returning to their ships. The poor buggers would need the fires but not the grog many would have brought along and hidden on the persons. He had never understood how they could be so clever about something such as hiding grog and so foolish not to think they would be discovered drinking. He prayed there would be no snow during the night.

There was no volley from the soldiers, nor was there a cheer. Something was amiss. The oxcarts bearing the cannon were in sight. He decided not to wait but before he turned to go up the road a voice called, "Beg pardon Sir." It was Bullard the corporal of marines. "Major Ellington's compliments, the fort is abandoned!"

"Abandoned!" Donland exclaimed.

"Aye Sir. Major Ellington is moving some of the men into the fort. He said the guns were spiked."

"Well!" Donland said and was surprised he had spoken.

Sumerford slapped him on the back and smiled. "No battle this day, eh?"

Donland found Ellington and Seviers in the office of the fort's commander. There was a roaring fire in the fireplace and the chill was already off the room.

"I suppose they saw us coming and decided to run. The colonials round about here are farmers and merchants, not soldiers. When they saw the army coming up the road they went home," Seviers stated.

"Fortunate for them," Ellington said. "My men were spoiling for a good set-to."

"Fortunate for us as well," Donland replied. "It gives us time to get Captain Furman on his way unmolested. But, I fear word will have reached the commanders of the militia and they will be alerted to our presence and send more seasoned troops. As I remember the map of this area, the wagons are to cross a ferry some ten miles north of here. Is that so?"

"Yes, Port Royal ferry across Whale Branch," Seviers answered.

Donland considered the information and made his decision, "Night will be upon us in a couple of hours. Major Ellington will have his troops ready to march at first light."

He turned to Jackson, "Mister Jackson you will see to our men that they are fed and housed. Send a runner back to instruct Captain Powell and Captain Newland to put to sea as soon as their cargoes are ashore."

"Is that wise?" Seviers asked.

"I believe it is. We can't afford a chance discovery by an enemy frigate or larger vessel while anchored. The ships need to be at sea as soon as possible. My first priority is the ships and men under my command. They shall be at sea where they can maneuver as needed. We will go with you to the ferry and send word back to my ship where we can be retrieved. Your wagons should arrive here before dark. How long will it take for them to reach the ferry?"

"Three hours providing we meet no opposition," Seviers answered.

"There will be none!" Ellington stated.

"Why so Major?" Seviers asked?

The question alerted Donland that something was amiss between the Ellington and Seviers.

"Why so?" Donland asked.

Ellington thrust out his chest and his chin. "My men will sweep away any opposition between here and the ferry, of that I am quite certain. After that Captain Furman is entirely on his own."

"That is according to our orders," Donland stated.

"But Sir," Seviers blurted. "You are to assist me until those wagons reach Colonel Boyd."

Now Donland saw the rub. Major Ellington and his troops were to return aboard the sloops and be delivered to Savannah. They were only to assist the landing of the munitions and supplies. Ellington well knew his orders. Advancing on the fort and seeing the wagons to the ferry fell under assisting. What Seviers was inferring was that Ellington and his men were to come under his command. Ellington was having none of it.

It was Sumerford who spoke, "Major Ellington has his orders, as does Captain Donland. We shall set you upon your way but once away you will be on your own. Let there be nothing more said to this end."

"Aye," Donland said.

Ellington was satisfied, it showed in his smug smile. Seviers would be on his own.

Sumerford decided to take his leave. "There is little else for me here. There are other matters I need to attend to."

"Such as?" Donland asked.

Sumerford replied, "Someone has to watch over the wagons."

Donland doubted that was Sumerford's purpose but thought it best not to pursue the question.

Sumerford again smiled; a smile Donland knew meant deceit. Whatever his plans, they would not be disclosed.

Chapter Seven

During the night the clouds cleared. Donland was thankful for the bed with the straw mattress and goose-feather pillow. He slept through the night and was awakened by Honest before daylight. The room was cozy warm and there was the smell of bacon. He roused and dressed feeling refreshed. If the day progressed as he imagined, he would be back aboard *Hornet* before nightfall.

Major Ellington had his men formed up in ranks inside the fort when Donland came out. The sun was just beginning to brighten the eastern sky. Light clouds to the north hinted at a total clearing, already it was much warmer than the day before.

"Good morning Captain Donland," Ellington said as Donland approached.

The major was wearing a clean uniform and was freshly shaved. Donland felt somewhat drab in comparison.

Jackson joined them looking as fresh as Ellington.

"Where are our men?" Donland asked.

"I sent them out on the road half-hour ago. Mister Aldridge and Booth, Captain Powell's midshipman is with them awaiting orders."

"I've sent my scouts out as well," Ellington said.

"Are you ready to march?" Donland inquired.

"All accounted for and ready to march," Ellington answered.

"In that case we shall be about it," Then to Seviers he said, "We will expect you and Captain Furman at the ferry after mid-day."

As an after thought he turned back to Major Ellington." Leave five of your men to assist Major Seviers and to act as runners. The colonials may return or raise a force from the town."

"That they may. I shall attend to it Captain Donland," Ellington answered.

"Captain Pellew!" Ellington bellowed to his second in command.

Honest silently joined the group. "Beg pardon Captain, word if you please."

"Aye," Donland replied and stepped away from Ellington and Seviers.

Honest spoke quietly and Donland listened then nodded. "As quick as you can," He replied.

Seviers did not miss the interruption. "Where's your man off to?"

Donland said evenly, "An errand for me."

Ellington returned, "Ready Sir!"

"Very well, let us be about today's needs."

Major Ellington, Donland and Captain Pellew led the

column along the road until the outskirts of Beauford where they halted when one of the scouts met them and reported to Ellington.

"More than a company!" The Scout stated. "They are setting up defenses at the edge of town.

Ellington seemed to swell, "By God we shall rout them!"

"What's your name?" Donland asked.

"Willis Sir!" The solider answered hesitantly.

"Willis do they have cannon with them?"

"Not that I seen Sir, mostly just farmers though."

"We'll crush them!" Ellington said with glee. "Captain Pellew!" he bellowed to summon his second in command.

Donland ignored the bluster. "Willis are there other roads leading out of the town to the east?"

"Yes Sir."

Ellington was busy giving Pellew orders and had not heard the question or answer.

"Major Ellington we shall advance to the east and avoid the colonials," Donland said flatly. "Let us move with haste, and as quietly as possible."

"Whhhaatt?" Ellington exploded.

"You heard my order. We will advance to the east and avoid the colonials."

"But Sir, I must protest. We are more than a match for the bloody farmers."

"Major!" Donland raised his voice. "Experienced military men lead those so-called farmers. The men under them have been trained. I do not know how they are equipped but I can assure you that they are not mere farmers. We shall avoid a fight!"

Ellington's face was a deep red and he stated, "I now know where you sympathies lie!"

Jackson stepped between them.

"Lieutenant!" Donland shouted.

Jackson turned toward Donland and seeing the look in his eye withdrew.

Donland's anger was evident. "My loyalties Major Ellington are to the king, the navy and my admiral who has ordered me to deliver you and your troops to Savannah. He did not order me to deliver corpses. I will follow his orders and you will follow mine or I will have you relieved of your command! Is that understood?"

Ellington was at least twenty years older and thirty pounds heavier than Donland. They stood eye to eye, however, neither blinked.

"Runner coming Sir!" Pellew inserted.

Both Donland and Ellington turned away toward the runner.

"Captain Powell's compliments Sir," the runner managed. "*Stinger* is cruising off Hilton Head with *Hornet* and *Jacket* in her lee. He will return to Land's End in mid-afternoon to take you off."

The sloops were in good hands with Powell in command. Once the wagons were safely away, the sloops would be waiting.

"Report to Mister Booth," Donland ordered the runner.

Seviers asked, "May I make a suggestion Captain Donland."

"I would welcome it," Donland replied.

"Since you do not want to fight, I assume you do not want to be perused either?"

"Aye," Donland said.

"Might it be feasible to have Major Ellington, dispatch twenty-five men and send them at the run to circle behind the colonials. Have them make as much noise as they can to draw their attention. Captain Pellew can command them. They won't engage and will retreat toward the ferry and hide once the colonials take the bait. We can continue along the east road and find a suitable path to the ferry."

Ellington looked as if he would again protest but he refrained.

"Make it so Major," Donland said.

Pellew and his party set off at a run a few minutes later. Ellington was still steaming after returning from instructing Pellew. One hard look from Donland settled the issue of command. He was ready and willing to make it clear that he was in command of the expedition. One thing he had learned in his years of serving in ships was that command could not and should not entertain dissention. There could be only one commander and his orders from Admiral Rowley gave him that authority. Ellington for all his bluster understood. He could fume but there was nothing he could do except be shot for mutiny or hung for treason. At that moment, Donland would do either if it came to it.

The column moved at a snail's pace. The track was soft and spongy. Men put their shoulders to the wheels to move the heavy wagons along. Donland had arranged soldiers to the front, wagons in the middle and the seaman behind. It was the seamen who were tasked to keep the wagons moving. They shouldered their burdens without complaint. Two miles along the track Donland was forced to call a halt.

Endicott, a wiry young man from Virginia, was out of breath as he ran up to Donland. "Message Sir!" He said and handing over a folded note.

The note was from Dewitt. "Orders to stand off Hilton Head until later in the day. Powell and Newland are two miles out. All is well."

"Any trouble?" Donland asked the young man.

"None sir!" He answered and added, "Mister Dewitt sent me and four lads ashore before night in your gig. We're to keep watch and warn you if enemy ships are sighted."

Donland felt better knowing a line of communication existed. He could only pray that the other part of his planning came to fruition. The longer they stayed on land the greater the risk. If at all possible he wanted this business concluded before nightfall.

A red-coated soldier hurried up to Donland and saluted.

"Captain Pellew's compliments sir," the man said. His uniform was caked in mud and he had a bloody gash over his right eye.

"Wounded?" Donland asked.

The solider immediately put his hand to his brow, he grinned. "No sir, bloody Dan Smith loosed a tree limb, whipped right cross my noggin and put me in the mud."

Donland returned the grin and asked, "What's the message?"

"The colonials stopped their advance and are moving back toward the town. Captain Pellew requests orders."

"How far away are your mates?"

"Mile, maybe a mile and a half, beyond that big tree over there. Ain't nothing but swamp twixt here and there. I was up to my belly most of the way."

Donland pulled the map he had brought along from his pocket. There was no road in the direction of Pellew. It would be impossible to get wagons through the swamps. The map did show a road along the river that seemed to end where the marshes began or at the river's edge. The problem was there was no route connecting to the ferry. He would have to chance finding solid ground for the wagons or be forced to return to the Beauford road.

"Have you reported to Major Ellington?" Donland asked.

"No sir, Captain Pellew gave me strict orders to report to you first."

"Get some rest and some food," Donland said and considered what Pellew had done. The man was not a dimwit and understood what they were to be about. Fighting a battle for no apparent reason was a fool's game but Ellington would not see it.

Jackson came over. "We've a man that's lived around here."

"Does he know of a road to the ferry?" Donland asked.

"Don't know Sir, name's Campbell."

"Ask him if the river road up ahead goes to the ferry."

Ellington was striding along the wagons. Donland hoped no one had told him about the runner from Pellew. The look on the man's face was that of a storm about to break.

"Nothing ahead but a river!" Ellington bellowed. "We've got to go back to the road and form up for a fight!"

It was not what Donland wanted. But he also knew that the colonials would be sending more troops. His small force would fare poorly against what was already present and additional troops would make his task impossible. Ellington was right in wanting to fight now but Ellington was not considering the cost of the fight. They might win but only to have to withdraw and lose the wagons.

Donland again pulled the map from inside his greatcoat and unfolded it. "There is a track or road here," he said and indicated it. "I don't know if it ends at the river or in the swamp. Whichever the case, it is at least two miles short of the ferry. Perhaps it extends, perhaps it doesn't. We shall send a runner to find out."

"That's it! You are just going to sit here, trapped!" Ellington exploded.

"No!" Donland shot back and continued loud enough for those around to hear, "Major rejoin your men and await orders!"

Ellington glared, furled his bottom lip and strode off.

Jackson returned along with the man Campbell. "Campbell said he doesn't know but he's willing to run ahead and report back."

Donland rubbed his chin, thought and decided. "You there!" He called to the soldier from Pellew.

The man came over.

"I want you to go with Campbell to the end of this road and there will be a track leading off to your right. Maybe a road maybe nothing more than a path. You report back to Captain Pellew and have him rejoin with Major Ellington. You may well be wading swamps again. Campbell you'll return if the road runs out. But before you return, look about for some means to get those wagons to the ferry. Understood?"

"Okay if that's what you want!" Campbell answered.

"Off you go then!"

The two men set off at a trot. Jackson leaned in toward Donland. "We're trapped if there's no road."

"Aye," Donland whispered.

Donland's watch showed a quarter after twelve. They were running out of time. Campbell and the solider had been gone close to an hour. Darkness would come upon them in less than five hours. That was all the time he had to get those wagons across the ferry. By morning, the colonials would have cut off all escape routes.

He saw Honest approaching with a black man following. Donland smiled.

"I'm Captain Donland," he introduced himself.

"Bartholomew Freeman," Honest's companion announced.

"I take it that you were a slave?"

"Naw Sir, I was born free but lives in the swamp away from all them slavers."

Donland smiled and asked, "Do you know this swamp?"

"Yes Sir, I know it better that any man about here."

Donland took out his map and held it out for Bartholomew to see. "We want to go to the ferry there," he pointed. "Is there anyway to get there from here?" Again he indicated with his finger.

"Naw sir but there be a way when the tide be down along the creek."

Donland studied the map but did not see a creek. It was low tide; that he did know.

"Why can we go by the creek?" Donland asked.

"Coral and rock it is; little sand."

It made sense, an old coral reef this far inland would be solid enough for wagons.

"Bartholomew will you guide us?"

"Yessur'."

Chapter Eight

The old coral reef was solid enough but little more than a game trail wide. Donland set the men to work with axes, machetes and even swords to clear cane, pine and scrub oak to make it passable for the wagons. Bartholomew moved ahead of the column and used poles to mark the path that needed to be cut. At one point they had to resort to digging and filling a large hole. The soldiers laughed at the seaman's hard labor until Donland ordered them to rotate a turn pushing wagons. No one laughed after that.

Splashing drew Bartholomew's attention. He held up a hand, and the word was passed to be quiet. The soldiers found their muskets and began to prepare them.

There were voices and more splashes.

Donland heard Pellew shout, "Harkness move your arse!"

It was a welcome voice.

Pellew and his men waded up to solid ground, and he grinned as he saw Donland.

"How did you locate us?" Donland asked.

Pellew grinned, "A deaf man could hear all those trees being cut and all that yelling to heave and push."

At that answer Donland had to ask, "What of the colonial militia, are they following you?"

"We've led them on a merry chase, I divided my men into three parties and each was instructed to show themselves at different locations. We confused them and they're chasing their tails. But no, they are not following. We only just entered the swamp when we caught sight of the wagons. The road to the ferry is no more than five chains from where we stand."

"You've done exceptionally well Captain. I'm in your debt," Donland stated.

"Sir, there is a problem." Pellew said flatly. "The water at the ferry is low, and the ferry is stuck on a mud bank."

Donland blew a breath. "That is a problem. The colonials will have a guard there, eventually. The tide is just now beginning to flood. Be near dark by the time there is enough water to re-float the ferry and move the wagons across. Looks like Major Ellington will have his battle after all."

"I could take twenty fresh men and guard the ferry." Pellew suggested.

"Aye," Donland answered. "Do so."

Ellington was advancing toward them.

Donland gauged the situation and said, "Be off Captain, I shall send Major Ellington on your heels with the rest of your redcoats."

"Where the bloody hell are you sending my men off to now?" Ellington demanded.

"You're going to get your battle Major. I've sent Captain Pellew to guard the ferry until you and your remaining force can cross the swamp and set up a defensive line.

"That's more like it Sir! By thunder now you're about it!" Ellington said as he turned to leave.

"Major Ellington!" Donland called.

Ellington stopped and turned. "Beg pardon Sir!" He said and saluted.

Before Ellington could again set off Donland said, "Major you are to deploy your men out of sight and in the edge of the swamp. Do not form them up on open ground, that's an order."

Ellington wheeled, "I will not!"

"You will or I shall put Captain Pellew in charge and hold you here. Is that clear?"

Ellington was as enraged as a wounded bull. He did not reply and started off.

"Jackson take two men and see that he follows my orders, if he doesn't bind him and tell Captain Pellew that he is in command." Donland shouted loud enough for Ellington to hear.

They reached the road tired, exhausted and muddy. Across from where they met the road was the meadow, and the ferry was another hundred yards up the road. "Hurry along there!" Donland shouted. "No rest until we reach the ferry."

"Major Seviers and Captain Furman get those wagons to the ferry and ready to be loaded," Donland ordered. "We've not a moment to lose. I will see to the soldiers."

He was pleased to see that Ellington and Pellew had done as bidden. There was not a redcoat to be seen. The flat grassy meadow bordering the approach to the ferry contained a few scrub bushes but was empty of men. There would not be a battle if it were up to him. He prayed the colonials had enough sense not to try to cross the open ground.

Jackson and Bartholomew were waiting at the ferry.

"How long before we can get the ferry across?" Donland asked.

"It's stuck fast. An hour at least." Jackson answered.

"Waiting is out of the question," Donland said as he

gazed across to where the ferry was stranded. "Bend on a stout line and unhitch a yoke of oxen. See it you can pull it off that bank."

"Aye Captain."

"Bartholomew you know these woods and swamps, will you take one of my men to watch the road on the other side of that meadow to warn us when the colonials approach?"

"They come quiet. They knows these swamps as best as me. But I go."

"Honest you go with him."

"Aye Captain," Honest said and followed after Bartholomew.

"Weapons," Donland called after him. "Take swords and pistols."

He called to Dawkins, "Dawkins arm those men!"

A cheer rose from the men.

A runner from Jackson reported, "Beg pardon Captain they freed the ferry."

It was good news, now they could get the wagons across. The sooner they were away from the swamps and the colonials the better. He needed only a little more time. Looking up at the low gray sky he was keenly aware that darkness would overtake them long before they could get back aboard. The men were still wet from the swamp and would want to build fires. Donland could not and would not allow them to do so. They had to get the wagons across and get away or the colonials would surround them and capture them. There was neither time to build fires nor to rest.

They had brought no food, water or grog. The cold was setting in. Only those working to free the ferry were active. Those huddling beside the wagons for warmth were beginning to grumble. Fights were not far off. He needed those wagons on the ferry and his men away from here. The longer they were delayed the greater their peril. The men would fare poorly spending a night in the swamps; it would cost lives. The prudent thing would be to leave Seviers and Furman to getting the wagons across.

Jackson called, “Captain the ferry is across.”

“Is there enough water to float the wagons?” Donland asked.

“Half hour or more I'd say.” Jackson replied.

“That gives us less than three hours of daylight to get them across and our people away,” Donland observed.

Just then, Honest pushed through a group of men. He was breathing hard.

“The colonials?” Donland asked.

“Aye Captain,” Honest answered and sucked air into his lungs.

“We can't wait. Jackson start loading the ferry if nothing else we shall haul it across by hand, we have enough men. I shall see to the army; they must hold.” Donland started off followed by Honest.

They trotted the hundred yards to the meadow. To Donland’s horror, Major Ellington had his command formed up in ranks and was well into the meadow.

“Major Ellington I ordered you to form a perimeter in the edge of the swamp, we are not here for a battle if it can be avoided!”

“We shall not cower in the face of the enemy Captain Donland!” Ellington shot back.

“Captain Pellew!” Donland shouted.

“He'll not answer you, he is being confined,” Ellington stated. “The man will be broken!”

Donland's anger raged. “You Sir are the one that will suffer. You have disobeyed my orders and if we live, you sir, will be brought up on charges of mutiny!”

Ellington said nothing. He remained impassive.

“Very well Major you leave me no choice. You are relieved!”

Ellington faced Donland. He laughed. “You have not the authority nor the support.”

Donland pulled the pistol from his belt. There was too much at risk for this man's bluster. In one swift movement he raised the pistol and brought the barrel down across the side of Ellington's skull. The major dropped without a sound.

"Into the wood!" Donland ordered! The men gaped but none moved.

"Move your arses! Now!" He shouted and there was the shuffle of feet but none broke rank.

"You there!" Donland pointed his pistol at a sergeant. "Bring Captain Pellew!"

"You two!" The sergeant said to two men, "Bring the Captain."

The two men looked to one another then broke rank and obeyed.

"Sergeant take charge of the major," Donland ordered. To the ranks of men he commanded, "Fall back into the wood."

They began to move, slowly at first then the sergeants took over pushing and cursing.

"Fire!" A voice shouted from the other side of the meadow and instantly there was a volley and plumes of musket smoke. Balls crashed around Donland but none struck him or any other man.

"Form up!" A voice shouted.

Donland hurried to the safety of the wood and sheltered behind a large pine tree. Captain Pellew fell beside him.

"Captain Pellew have your men fire independent. Keep them behind cover," Donland said to him.

Ranks of men could be seen coming through the smoke in the fading light.

Pellew stood, "Independent fire! Mark them down!" he shouted.

Muskets began to crack. Smoke began to fill the air; it became as thick as fog hugging the ground. The advancing ranks faltered.

"Hold fire!" Pellew commanded.

The firing slowed and then stopped.

Donland saw intermittent movement through the smoke. The colonials seemed to be withdrawing.

“They'll reform,” Pellew said.

“Aye but you must hold,” Donland said and added. “I must see to the ferry. The wagons will be across soon. When the last one is across, we will leave this place. Should be no more than two hours.”

“Back through the swamps in the dark?” Pellew asked.

Donland hated to answer the man but he gave the best answer he could. “That is yet to be determined but we will get your men back to the ships.”

“Very good Sir. I've had my belly of mud and cold.” Pellew said.

Donland had gone twenty yards when there was the crash of a volley followed almost instantly by a second. As long as the colonials attempted to cross the meadow in ranks they would be marked down. Donland thought it odd how the roles of the colonials and the soldiers had reversed. It was the redcoats firing from cover and the colonials marching in rank into merciless fire. He was thankful that Pellew was a better solider than Ellington or their efforts would have been wasted.

The ferry was moving. The breath of the men standing about was thick in the cold. It took Donland a minute or more to locate Jackson.

“We haven't much time,” Donland stated.

“Aye, but we’ve enough to get the wagons across, no more than an hour. From the sound of the muskets I would venture the redcoats have their fight,” Jackson's voice held a hint of humor.

“Aye,” Donland managed. “We need to be away from this place as quickly as possible.”

“Back through the swamp or through the colonials?” Jackson asked.

Donland considered the question. He had framed it in his mind when coming from Pellew. He had no answer then, and he had none now. This was not a place he wanted any to die.

"That man, Bartholomew, is he still with us?"

"Aye, there," Jackson said and pointed to a group of men huddled behind a wagon.

The men had blankets. Donland assumed the blankets had been in the wagon. He'd not fault the men.

There was no way but to ask straight out. "Bartholomew is there a way around the meadow without passing through the swamps?"

"Be a creek to cross, no road, no path," Bartholomew answered.

"But there is a way, a way for all these men?" Donland asked.

"Men yes but not no wagons, trees is thick down yonder."

"Will you guide us?"

"If you want."

"Yes, we need to be away from this place."

Donland could do nothing more but wait as the ferry went across and returned. Time was slipping away. The firing from the meadow had ceased. Only the occasional musket shot signaled that there was anyone in the gloom beyond them. Captain Pellew was holding but for how long against a force that was being reinforced with fresh men?

The rain returned; a slow soaking rain that held bits of ice. Donland felt that he had never been so cold in his life. He knew his men were feeling the same. Each would be longing for a tot of grog, warm clothes and the warmth of their hammocks.

Two wagons remained. It was time.

"Mister Jackson you will accompany Bartholomew, we will begin our withdrawal. Form up into two ranks. The ones loading the wagons will follow when the wagons are away. Pass the word for silence. I shall stay until the last wagon is away."

"I'll be at your side," Sumerford said. Donland wasn't aware the man had joined him.

Major Seviers, muddy and wet was almost unrecognizable as he came out of the gloom. "Captain Donland we will be away shortly. Thank you Sir for your assistance. I wish you well on your passage back to your ship."

"Thank you Major Seviers. I trust your and our efforts have not been in vain. Please extend my compliments to Colonel Boyd."

"I will sir," Seviers answered and extended his hand.

Donland took the offered hand and Seviers hurried away.

"Matthias I will see Captain Pellew and have him make preparations to disengage from the militia. Please see to it that nothing hinders Major Seviers' crossing."

"That I will do," Sumerford answered.

Pellew was where Donland had last seen him. The wood was dark; were it not for the occasional flash of muskets Donland would not have seen the men hiding there.

"Captain we are withdrawing by a route to your right flank. The last wagon will be on its way in a few minutes. Once it is away, you will withdraw your men."

"Might I suggest sir that we route these blaggards first. Doing so will give us time to rejoin your people."

"Aye, you know your trade. I shall send a runner when we are ready."

Donland and Honest hurried through the dark wood back to the men at the ferry. He was pleased to find that the last wagon was on the ferry. Night had all but fallen and with it the temperature.

Sumerford was waiting on the road. "We will be left if we dawdle."

"Aye, let us rejoin our people." Donland answered.

"Isaac I am assuming you know the way even in the dark."

"Aye, the wood is no more than a hundred yards. From there we follow the edge of the water until we come to a small creek. We cross over. Bartholomew said we continue following the water on our right and will come to a track leading into the town."

"What of the colonials?" Sumerford asked.

"They'll camp at the meadow and wait until the dawn to attack."

"Poor buggers will have spent the night in the cold for nothing," Sumerford said.

"Aye!"

The bright flash of three muskets blinded them. Honest pulled Donland to the ground.

Sumerford pulled his pistol and fired, a scream answered his shot. Honest rose up and was among the attackers with his knife. A man yelled; another screamed in pain; Donland heard nothing.

Chapter Nine

He opened his eyes with great effort. He lay on his back in hay covered with blankets. He was warm. The light was dim, either cloudy or not yet day. He began to turn onto his side and felt a stabbing pain in his ribs; he sucked air to stifle the pain. Lying flat of his back he waited until the pain subsided and turned onto his other side. The pain was sharp but not unbearable. Moving his hand he discovered a bandage covered his torso.

Honest laid a hand across Donland's mouth. Their eyes met and the big man shook his head and put a finger to his lips. There was movement and Sumerford came into view, he was holding a pistol.

"They've gone," Sumerford stated.

Honest withdrew his hand and Donland asked, "Who?"

"Just some people, slaves."

"Honest get some water," Sumerford ordered.

Honest was but a moment until he returned and put a clay jug to Donland's lips.

Donland took a sip and decided he was thirsty. He

gulped three shallows.

“Where are we?” He asked.

“Garden's Corner, on the road to Charles Town.” Sumerford answered.

“Why?”

Sumerford grinned. “Your man Honest fought off five men and then carried you across the wash to the ferry landing. Seviers and his party were gone, so we hid in a barn. He bandaged you and I stole a mule. We only just stopped an hour ago.”

“How bad?” Donland asked wincing in pain.

“Not bad, tore a hole clean through just below the bottom rib. There will be a nasty scar I'm afraid,” Sumerford stated.

The shock must have shown on his face. A man shot with musket ball almost always died from blood poisoning. Only a skilled surgeon could save a man.

Sumerford shook his head. “You won't die. Honest won't let you. He put stuff on you and in you and washed it.”

Donland wasn't reassured. He understood why he was so warm; it was fever not the blankets. He lay back; he would be dead in two days. Betty's face came to him as he closed his eyes.

There was movement near him, he opened his eyes. Betty was there. He was dreaming. He remembered thinking of her and then nothing. He was dreaming.

“Darling Isaac,” she said as her face beamed.

“A dream,” he mumbled.

Her face became serious, “Oh, no. I'm here. Matthias brought you only this morning. You've been asleep and with the fever.”

His eyes closed. He felt her hand on his cheek. He opened his eyes; she was really there. Slipping a hand from under the covers he touched her face. A tear formed and ran down her cheek and landed on his bare chest. He drifted off to sleep once more.

"Mmph, better than it should be," Doctor Shillinglaw declared.

He probed a little more and Donland ignored the pain. "Wound is almost healed. No need for maggots. Another day of bed rest and you should be able to be up and about."

When the door closed Donland lifted the covers and slid out of bed. Before his feet hit the floor, Honest entered carrying trousers, a shirt, boots and a woolen coat. It was in his mind to ask for his uniform but he remembered that he was in Charles Town. They would hang him for a spy before sunset.

Being unconscious for days had puzzled him. He had seen men shot in the chest, in the shoulder and other parts of the body. Seen them hacked almost into but they had retained their wits. Sumerford had explained, "The first shot hit you and Honest yanked you down so hard that your head hit a tree root. Knocked the sense right out of you. I thought you were on your way to meet Saint Peter but when Honest routed those fellows he hoisted you up and we were away. I tried to stop him from going into the wash, damnable cold it was, but I couldn't stop him so I followed in after him. Stole that mule I told you about and the next day hired a coach. Cousin Betty was all a dither when she saw you."

The clothes felt good. They were new. Evidently Sumerford had a goodly purse about him. Everything fit which meant the clothes were tailored and someone had measured him while he slept. Knowing Matthias Sumerford as he did, he was not surprised to discover the uniform had been burned as not to risk the discovery of his identity. Honest too wore new clothes befitting an employee of a gentleman.

The uniform would have to be replaced when he rejoined *Hornet*. What of *Hornet*? Had Jackson reached her and set sail? He needed to talk with Sumerford about getting to *Hornet*, surely the man had means of getting from Charles Town to Savannah. But would *Hornet* be there when he reached there?

"Ready Sir?' Honest asked.

"Aye," Donland replied. "A walk in the sunshine will be a tonic."

The sun shone brightly and there was a brisk wind on the veranda. His first steps had been tottery but Honest's strength had steadied him. The cold of Port Royal and the fever of the wound were forgotten as he settled into a fan-shaped chair in direct sun. Honest seated himself on a bench and crossed his legs. Donland considered how easily Honest had settled into the role. He wondered if Honest too longed for the seaman's life aboard *Hornet*? Surely he missed his young son and the boy would be worried about his father. David too, would most likely be worried.

"Enjoying the sun?" Sumerford asked.

"Aye!" Donland answered. "Whose house is this?"

"Mine," Sumerford answered. "I purchased it two years ago. Boston is delightful in the spring and fall but wretched in winter and summer."

"So, at this house there are no suspicions about you?"

"Unfortunately there are. As I come and go so often, there are questions. My arrival this time brought a visit from the provost. He was curious about Honest, wanted to know how he was employed and why he was not in the army. I explained that we were recently shipwrecked after being set upon by an English warship. It was a good thing you still did not have your wits. Your wound helped me convince him."

Donland changed tack. "It was thoughtful of you to buy the clothing."

"Not a bother, least I could do for the future husband of my dear cousin."

"And I suppose you explained that to the provost as well?"

"That I did and Betty confirmed it as the truth. So, the provost went off a happy fellow and with an invitation to the wedding."

"Again the wedding," Donland said.

"Yes, the wedding which I'm sure is in the offing. You should have seen how she fussed over you. Was it any other person in that bed she would have scarcely noticed. She would have been about her gowns, shoes and the like. No thought whatsoever of a dying man."

Inwardly, Donland was glad to hear of Betty's concern. Outwardly, it would not do to let it show. And, deep down inside he pushed it away because such concern conflicted with his duty.

There was a rustle of petticoats announcing Betty's approach.

"I shall leave you," Sumerford whispered and rose. He leaned closer, "I've sent word to Savannah that you are alive and will rejoin your ship."

Donland's eyes widened in shock. He was about to ask when they were leaving but Betty came into the room.

She seated herself in the chair opposite Donland. Once sitting, she ruffled her dress, smoothed it and placed her hands in her lap. She beamed at him and then her face became serious. "Will you stay until spring? Its only a few weeks away."

"I won't mislead you, my heart desires to stay but my duty is out there. When arrangements are made, I must go. We shall enjoy such time as we have in one another's company."

"Oh, Isaac it is not enough . . ."

"He broke in, "It is all we have, let us not spoil it with talk of leaving."

She sighed heavily. Their eyes met, and she said, "But"

and stopped.

Honest stood and walked to the garden wall. He pretended to be examining a small evergreen bush. It occurred to Donland that Honest once had a wife, a woman he probably loved very much. There was very little he knew about the man but in the days ahead before they returned to *Hornet* he would endeavor to know more. The man had, after all, saved his life while risking his own.

Betty brought him from his thoughts. "Isaac what does it mean, not this day, not this hour?"

"Where have you heard that phrase?" He asked.

"It was what you kept repeating sometimes when the fever held you."

He felt his face redden. His mind called up the faint image of Lieutenant Ellison. "Something I was taught at a very early age."

"But what does it mean? It must have been important for you to keep repeating it."

"The whole phrase is this, not this day, not this hour for others depend on me. I told you how Lieutenant Ellison rescued me from Mister Lillaby, the chandler. While serving with Ellison, there was a night that our ship was tossed about in a tremendous gale. He found me cowering, crying in the hold. I was terrified, and he did the most unusable thing for any officer. He drew me up, put his arms around me for the briefest of moments and whispered in my ear, 'Not this day, not this hour for others depend on me'. He then held me at arm's length and said, 'be afraid for only a fool is not but do your duty.' Then he said, repeat this, 'not this day, not this hour for others depend on me!' He kept saying it and we began shouting it. Since that night I've not forgotten and when fear comes to my heart, I repeat it."

Tears were in her eyes. She drew a handkerchief from her sleeve and wiped her tears. Glassy-eyed she said, "And even when the fever held you and you were afraid of dying you repeated it, even shouted it."

She wiped more tears, and he fought not to allow his emotion to show.

She beamed at him and said, "I am so glad I was able to share your life on the island and aboard the ship. I saw you as you are and not as you pretend to be. That is why I care so for you. It was so hard to write that letter and leave for Boston. I cried all the way there and only stopped when Matthias came to visit. He said to me, 'Foolish girl, when you love a man you love his life.' That's what I did, I started loving your life and not hating it. You love the sea; you love your ship. To love you, I must love what you love."

They sat in silence. Her words pierced his heart. They also had him in turmoil. Was he to love the things she loved, could he? His whole life had been about duty, about loyalty. But now, what place is there for love?

He used the arm of the chair to bear his weight as he stood. His body was still weak but it was to be ignored. He reached out his hands to her; she stood. He embraced her and nuzzled her neck. The smell of lavender stilled his mind. He held her and she him.

By the end of the first week, spring was in the air. There was no need for a coat. Donland felt strong. He had slept soundly, eaten well and was comforted with Betty's presence. They had walked, laughed and talked of places, people and things. They both avoided the future, of his leaving. He knew in his heart that he loved her and leaving her would rend his soul as surely as a sword a limb.

The first day of the next week a visitor came to the house, a man in fancy dress. Sumerford sat with the man in the library while Donland sat in the garden only a few steps from an open window. He overheard a few words as Sumerford and the man conversed. There was little doubt that the man was French. There were many French in Charles Town so his visit should have been no concern but the hushed tones of the conversation were a concern. Donland knew there was no value in asking Sumerford afterwards. The man kept his secrets and his dealings to himself.

Sumerford showed the man out and sought Donland. "Tomorrow at dawn," Sumerford simply said.

"By the Frenchman's ship?" Donland asked.

Sumerford laughed loudly then said, "Isaac you'd not make a good spy. You best stay with the navy and your ships." He laughed again.

There was no humor in Donland's tone. "Laugh if you will but as my life is in the balance, I should be told."

Sumerford clapped a hand on Donland shoulder. "He is loaning us his coach and giving me a letter from the French Counsel stating that I am to act on a matter in his behalf."

"But he is the enemy!" Donland protested.

Sumerford became serious. "And I am an agent of the King of England. As such, I make use of the resources available to me. Which includes the funds provided to obtain what I need to secure information. Not all men are as honorable as you Isaac."

Donland understood but understanding was not comfortable to his mind.

"Come, let us have a glass," Sumerford said. "Tomorrow we shall be bound for Savannah and the other love of your life. By the way, when is the wedding?"

It had taken time but Donland had learned the man. The question was clearly misdirection. He had to admit that Sumerford was right, there was no value in pursuing the conversation concerning the Frenchman. Sumerford would not share his secrets nor would he discuss his dealings with people like himself.

The wedding was very much on Donland's mind. He had avoided the subject with Betty and it had been between them as an invisible veil. Sumerford had on more than one occasion referenced marriage during their dinners and at other times. But Betty said nothing. It had fallen to Donland to fend off the question. But here, it was his last day in this house with her. It would be unfair to her to make any promise or even to allude to some future date. In his heart he was certain he wanted her for his wife but his head told it such was impossible; at least until this war ended.

Would he buy a house in New York should the English subdue the colonists? Or, would he buy a cottage in England on some fog-laden coast if the colonies became independent? Which would Betty choose? Perhaps Charles Town? London would be more to her liking. Would that be a possibility?

A home with Betty was desirable, his heart told him that. Reasoning told him that there were many obstacles to such a reality. She was waiting patiently for him to broach the subject but he could not. He had no answers; could offer her nothing. His heart desired her but he could not give in; not yet. When the war is over, then and only then could he began to hope to fulfill his passion.

She was waiting for him in his room. The lace curtain fluttered in the breeze. She sat in the upholstered beige wingback chair wearing a high-necked dress of emerald green. Her red hair glistened as a sunbeam struck it.

"Isaac you're leaving?" She asked.

He wanted with all his heart to say no. Seeing her sitting there she was more beautiful than in any dream of her he had ever had. "Aye," he whispered.

A tear appeared, and she quickly brushed it away. "I know Matthias has been seeing men at the house and I caught a few words. When will you go?"

He sighed and said, "Tomorrow." And quickly added, "I only learned of it this morning."

She looked down at her hands. "And as you should. Matthias keeps his secrets and his plans locked up inside. Sometimes I wonder if he even trusts himself in his sleep."

"You are close to him?" Donland asked.

"Yes," she answered. "We are more like brother and sister than cousins. His mother and father both died of fever.

My father was lost at sea. Before he died, he brought Matthias to live with us. So, we have lived in the same house all my life except when he was away at school."

"How is it that all the time we spent together on the island that you never spoke more than a few words about Matthias?" Donland asked.

She looked up at him. "He told me before he went away once that I should never tell anyone anything about him. He made me promise. I think he was already a spy then."

It was the first time the word spy had been brought to the forefront of conversation. Donland had come to think of Matthias only as the king's agent. In truth he was more than that, a spy and a pretender. It would not change their relationship. Matthias had more than earned his trust and he felt that perhaps he had earned the same from Matthias.

"He is the man he is," Donland said. "And, I think every man could say the same about himself if he is honest."

"Are you honest Isaac? Honest with me?" Her eyes were more pleading than her words.

"Yes, Betty oh, yes. I am honest with you for I can't be otherwise," he answered.

"Tell me then, you've never done so, do you love me?"

Her words went to his heart. He went to her and took her hands in his and she rose from the chair. He looked into her eyes and she into his. "I love you, I do," he said, and she threw her arms around him. His went around her shoulders and drew her close. The sweet smell of lavender filled his nostrils as they kissed.

At dinner, she cried and went to her room. Donland and Sumerford ate in silence. Even the good-natured Honest held his tongue. In the night the winter returned with the cold seeping in through the partially opened window. Donland rose to close it and he could hear her sobbing. His heart ached and sleep would not come to him until very late.

Chapter Ten

Dawn came; he dressed and joined Sumerford in the coach that would take them to Savannah. Honest sat beside the driver. Betty did not say goodbye.

Every few seconds he peered out the window in hopes she would see him off. His heart was heavy, and he imagined hers was as well. He concluded such was enough reason not to come down and wish him well.

"She has entrusted a letter to me," Sumerford said. "I'm to give it to you in Savannah and not before."

That would be her way thought Donland. Her tender heart was more comfortable with paper and ink. He would bide his time until Savannah two days hence.

The weather rebounded with afternoon warmth except for a brief afternoon shower. The cold of that day in Port Royal was a distant memory as was his struggle with death. Yet, there was heaviness in his heart. He'd not found an answer to his question. Could he love the things she loved?

He pondered that question as memories came and went; some replaced with daydreams.

It was just as well that he was lost in his thoughts and memories as a satchel of papers consumed Sumerford. It occurred to Donland to ask what was in the satchel as they boarded but decided better of it. Sumerford's secrets and his business were none of his affair. Betty and *Hornet* were all that mattered to him and were more than sufficient to occupy his mind. They wrote in silence until the driver reined up the horses.

Three men stood by a log lying across the road; a fourth was mounted on a plow horse without a saddle. Each was armed with a musket, a pistol in his belt and a long knife hanging at his side. They were not highwaymen but local militia.

The one with a long drooping mustache approached the coach window. "Beg your pardon gentleman but do you have papers?"

"Yes," Sumerford answered and handed the envelope containing the Frenchman's letter through the window.

The man took the envelope and pulled the folded paper from it. He read and then replaced the letter in the envelope and handed back to Sumerford. "Frenchie eh?" he asked.

"No dear sir, just on business for the French government."

"You have to pay the toll anyway, government or no government."

"How much?" Sumerford asked?

"Ten dollars in paper or ten shillings," the man said without hesitating.

Sumerford did not reply or move. He stared straight at the man for thirty seconds or more then said, "I shall be returning along this road in two days. I shall pay your toll today and when I pass this way two or three days from now do not ask for it again."

The man opened his mouth but then closed it. Sumerford held out three Spanish doubloons. The man took the money and stepped back. He eyed the money for a few seconds then looked into Sumerford's eyes.

Donland also saw the man's eyes, and they reflected greed. Then suddenly they changed to fear. He glanced at Sumerford who was holding a pistol pointed at the man's head.

"Shall we pass?" Sumerford asked.

"Move the log Henry he paid," the mustached man shouted.

Henry kicked the horse's ribs and pulled the log from the road. The coach driver did not hesitate and started the horses forward.

In parting Sumerford said, "I shall pass this way again in two or three days. Remember that I paid the toll and remember I will not be trifled with."

Donland smiled. He knew, as did Sumerford, that the gold would be spent, the man drunk and some woman bedded. The man would not be taking any more tolls and would lucky not to be hanged by the commander of the militia for desertion. But, in this instance, it was better to pay than to fight.

They stopped for the night at Garden's Corner. The inn, a white wood-framed building with a shake roof, offered one room upstairs and another in the back of the house. Donland and Honest shared the upstairs-unheated room and the walls were unpainted lats.

"Will be a cold night Captain," Honest observed.

"Aye," Donland answered. "But not our first nor our last."

"True Sir," Honest replied.

The food was simple fare but hot. They dined on ham, beans, potatoes and fresh bread. The innkeeper provided ale. Following the meal the men gathered in the kitchen, as there was no drawing room, and smoked cigars and drank corn-based liquor.

Donland did not feel the cold, and he doubted that Honest did. He awoke with a terrible thirst and an aching head. Ice had formed in the top of the pitcher of water and he skimmed it off. The freezing water quenched his thirst but did nothing for his aching head. He decided to avoid such drink in the future.

Sumerford greeted them at daybreak as they came down for breakfast. "Eat plenty for we shall not eat again till we reach Savannah this evening," Sumerford instructed.

Before them the innkeeper's wife placed eggs, ham, biscuits and chicory coffee.

"You've made this passage before?" Donland asked.

Matthias only smiled and pushed a fork of eggs into his mouth.

Donland shook his head in wonderment. Sumerford gave nothing up.

The driver slowed as they came to the New River Bridge some twenty miles from Garden's Corner. Two men stood in the roadway with pistols in their belts. The driver drew up several hundred feet from the men.

Sumerford looked out, saw the men and said to the driver, "Drive on I shall deal with them."

The two men separated and came to opposite sides of the horses. Donland felt something jab him in the ribs and when he looked down, he saw one of Sumerford's pistols. He took it and cocked it.

The highwaymen made no pretense of collecting tolls. "Hands on your heads," A burly man with a full very dirty beard demanded. He held a cocked pistol in one hand and with the other reached to open Sumerford's door.

Sumerford began raising his arms and when his pistol cleared the window he fired into the man's face. The man's pistol exploded, and the ball buried itself in the coach roof.

Donland kicked the coach door open into the other man. He did not fall but staggered backward. Donland raised the pistol and fired hitting the man in the chest. Instantly he leapt from the coach and jerked the pistol from the man's grip.

The ball had torn into the man's right chest. Blood and foam began erupting from the man's lips.

"He's done for Captain," Honest said from above Donland.

"Let us be away before some passer-by takes notice of us," Sumerford said.

Donland obeyed and climbed into the coach and the driver lashed out at the horses. They began a fast trot.

"Don't fret. I've killed my share of their like," Sumerford said and added. "Billingsley is well used to my ways. He will have us miles from here before there are questions."

The coach rumbled onto the bridge. Before it reached the other end, three men scrambled up the bank and onto the road. They were arms with pistols.

"Sumerford!" Billingsley shouted when he spotted the men.

Sumerford pulled another pistol and leaned from the window.

A pistol fired, and the ball threw splinters into the coach. One stuck into the upper arm of Sumerford.

The horses reared as one of the men began waving a blanket." We'll have to fight the buggers!" Sumerford shouted.

Donland drew his sword, opened the door and leaped out. A thin man with a sagging hat thrust a bayonet at him. He parried it aside, spun and slashed the man across the neck.

There were two pistol shots and screaming. Honest leapt from the box with knife in hand and stood beside Donland. The horses shied and Billingsley fought to control them. It was then that Donland saw Sumerford on his knees.

He threw himself under the coach, rolled and came up in time to lash out at a man with a sword poised to strike

Sumerford. He blocked the blow and fell backward. The man's eyes first widened in triumph but then changed to horror as Honest's knife struck him in the side.

"Thank you for that!" Sumerford said as he gained his feet.

Two other men lay in the road writhing in pain. One tried to stand but fell to the ground clawing at the frozen dirt.

"Are you injured?" Donland asked.

"I think not." Sumerford answered. "Bloody horse knocked me down when I fired at the second one and missed. But for you, he would have had me."

Donland smiled, "Aye and you'd missed the wedding. But were it not for Honest we'd both miss it."

"He's good with a knife," Sumerford said.

"Aye, and more," Donland said appreciatively.

"Highwaymen common here about?" Donland asked as they were again traveling

Sumerford smiled. "Yes and a fine coach such as this one brings them out of their pits. But, we should not be troubled for the remainder of our travel as there are more people about."

Once the coach settled into a rhythm, Sumerford began to clean and load his pistols.

Donland studied Matthias. The man was secretive and methodical. He was taking great care cleaning the pistols, loading and then polishing. It was as though he wanted to leave nothing to chance; no possibility of malfunction or misfire. When he needed those pistols, he would expect them to perform to perfection. He was a man who could kill without regret. Donland concluded that he would do well to remember that fact.

Sumerford put away the pistols and took up the satchel again. He was soon immersed in the documents. Donland turned his attention to the countryside. There was little to see except tall pine, scrub oak and the occasional beaver pond.

There was nothing green other than the pines. The world outside the window was a bleak brown; he closed his eyes and imaged he could smell the salt of the sea and feel the rush of wind. He was not aware he slept.

The coach slowed and Donland came awake.

"I was about to wake you," Sumerford stated. "We're turning onto Canal Street."

Donland raised himself and turned to the window. It was almost dark. They passed all manner of buildings from warehouses to foundries. The smell of rotting fish was very strong, and he supposed it to be low tide. Occasionally, in the dim light, he thought he could see the river. He would not know where *Hornet* lay.

"I have rooms at a very good inn near the waterfront. The food is the best in Savannah and the beds are the softest this side of Boston. We'll send word to your ship to fetch you in the morning," Sumerford said.

"Aye," Donland agreed.

He was anxious to be aboard but the lateness of the day prevented it. He would have to contend with one last night ashore.

The coach stopped in front of a three-story elegant brick building. Gaslights burned in front of magnificent white columns reaching from the cobblestones to the roof. Three men in matching livery hurried to help them from the coach and retrieve their luggage.

Stepping into the hall was like stepping into a palace. Donland had seen some very fine houses in New York and Boston but this inn in Savannah surpassed them all. Chandeliers hung from the ceilings and gaslights burned in cornices. Marble topped all the tables and the coat racks were fine mahoganies. The floor was a pattern of gray and white marble.

"Don't concern yourself," Sumerford said. "Our rooms are paid for, it is the least our masters can do for us." He grinned.

Donland was aware that Honest had followed them into the hall. He said to him, "See if any of our people are in the town. You'll know where to look," He took out his purse.

"I'll not need money," Honest said.

"Aye, you'll not but the inn-keeper will need a coin or two. You may be awhile before you find a mate about, I'd not want you to not buy him a tot."

"Thank you kindly," Honest said as he accepted the money.

Sumerford said, "A bath before dinner will not come amiss. I feel as though I've enough dirt and dust on me to fill the hold of your ship."

"A bath!" Donland exclaimed. "It's winter man, you'll have your death!"

"On the contrary, the water is heated as is the room. All the luxury of a king is yours for this night. Enjoy, you've more than earned it," Sumerford said as he clapped Donland on the back. "And I do owe you, you saved my life back there on the road and I'll not forget it."

Donland shook his head. "No Matthias, if anything that was payment for the many times I feel you saved mine. Your care of me in Charles Town alone is more debt than I can ever repay."

"Debt! Let us not speak of debt for there is none and will never be such between us," Sumerford said in sincerity.

Sirs!" A man dressed very formality and wearing a white powdered wig said.

Donland and Sumerford both turned in the man's direction.

"Your rooms are prepared. Please be so kind as to continue your conversation there. Please gentlemen follow the porter to your rooms," the man with the wig urged.

The rooms were furnished with heavy white drapes with beige stripes, a thick beige quilted coverlet, and thick feather beds. Two upholstered chairs in beige brocade sat in front of a well-tended fireplace.

"Isaac you should be comfortable here. Not as comfortable as perhaps you would be in your bed in your cabin but comfortable enough," Sumerford said. "I shall be across the hall and we will dine in two hours if that is suitable to you."

Donland stood staring at the room. "Aye," he answered without looking at Sumerford.

Sumerford had turned to go to his room and Donland called after him. "Matthias."

Sumerford had his hand on the doorknob.

"There was something you were about to say before the clerk interrupted. Something about debt? You said there would be none between us."

Sumerford's face seemed to go tight. "I've not wanted to say it now but I will. Isaac, there are few men who have placed unquestionable trust in me or have extended friendship as you have. These months since you rescued me from the jungle we have served together and fought together. You've valued my advice. Your sense of duty and loyalty have caused me to think long and deep about my own values," he paused. "That said, there can be no debt between us. I look forward to the day of your wedding to my dear cousin and I gladly receive you as a brother."

Sumerford turned abruptly and opened his door. He did not look back.

Morning sunlight slipped through the crack in the drapes. Donland awoke slowly enjoying the warmth and softness of the bed.

"Morning Captain," Honest said from one of the chairs.

"Morning Sir," David said from the other chair. Behind him stood Simon Vickers, Honest's son.

Slowly Donland sat up. He was aware that he was wearing a nightshirt the innkeeper supplied. It had been some time since he had awoken to be wearing anything other than breeches and shirt.

He rubbed his eyes and focused. He sighed and said, "Gentlemen be about your duties!"

Honest and the boys looked to one another and then Honest laughed. "We are Captain!"

After breakfast Donland and Sumerford walked through the streets to the quay. *Hornet* and *Stinger* were anchored in the roads. He saw them as they neared the river.

"Here," Sumerford said and extended an envelope. "This is as far as I go. I've my own duties to attend."

Donland extended his hand. "We've done well together. Might we serve together at a later time?"

"Isaac, another time will come," Sumerford said as he grasped Donland's hand.

He watched Sumerford walk away and then remembered the envelope. There was about it the smell of lavender.

"To my love, I love the things you love," she had written on it. Her intent, he was sure, was to reassure him that her love had not faltered.

He looked out across the quay to *Hornet*. She was his love and his love loved her.

Made in the USA
Columbia, SC
02 November 2020